Demeter's Fall

Demeter's Fall

a novel by

by Kevin Hulit

Demeter's Fall

For
Wayne

1

When Carson Quest discovered the secret that would one day end the world it was completely by chance. Standing on a ridge that overlooked several cornfields, he was overseeing test trials for an experimental fertilizer he developed for his company, GroQuest, that doubled as an erosion blocker. The product was being tested on leased land in a rural town called Denton. Carson chose the field mainly for its subtle inclined pitch, which was necessary for testing the product. The land gradually crept uphill over the course of a few hundred yards, butting up against a ridge on the north end. Keller Farm sprawled out on the other side.

The Sun was setting, and as it sunk toward the horizon it cast its orange glow over the fields. Carson basked in the waning light as his face turned into the gentle winds that ushered in the night. The caress of the warm midsummer breeze on his skin felt tranquil, but after a deep serene exhale Carson opened his eyes and caught a glimpse of an anomaly in the fields on the far end of Keller Farm. A self-taught man of science, it piqued his curiosity.

Working fields in Denton was nothing unordinary for Carson. He had spent years there, developing a large line of commercial grade fertilizers used all over the world, which had made him a millionaire, and he spared no expense enriching his passion for science with seemingly endless ventures to research and develop every idea his mind could muster. Seeing the odd condition of Frank Keller's field was an opportunity for discovery that, as a scientist, he couldn't pass up. Alone on the ridge, surrounded by nothing but acres of cornfields, he hiked down to Keller's field for a closer look at the unusual crop layout he had spotted. The field was planted in linear rows as any other cornfield would be, except for a section near the middle that appeared to be barren in a kind of geometric way. A pattern made up of a series of circles, all varying in size, linked together like a chain and ran north and south through the middle of the field. Upon reaching the oddity, Caron discovered that the soil in the strange crop formation was charred and hot. The only explanation he could conjure for the source of the heat was that it must have been from below the surface, perhaps a recent change in geothermal activity; the formation of a new volcano or a long-forgotten coal mine fire advancing under the field. He saw no evidence of a fire or lightning strike, nor had he seen any while working the adjoining field all week. The patterning in the field simply wasn't consistent with that type of event anyhow. Whatever the cause, it was something rare.

After a few days of preparations, he mounted a solitary midnight excursion to the hot zone; no employees to manage and no Kellers working around the farm. He returned to the field with a small, treaded machine used for well drilling that he had modified so that it would drill horizontally instead of vertically, and wasted no time setting up the machine on the edge of the mysterious, simmering crop circles. He started drilling a tunnel below the surface along the north-south path the irregularity seemed to travel. The tunnel was narrow, but wide enough to feed an inspection camera through. He expected to see evidence of a newly formed volcanic shaft or possibly a hot spring or geyser, but was astounded when he saw what looked like small pieces of sheet metal in the camera's video feed. The Keller family had owned this land for generations, and Carson was betting that Frank knew what was under the ground but chose to sit on it, keeping it hidden away. Whatever rested under that burning field had been an energy source strong enough to scorch the earth immediately above it. Its secrecy agitated Carson's acute desire for omniscience, and as he looked at the pieces of metal discovered by the inspection camera, he vowed to unearth what Keller was hiding. He planned to go back to the site just after sunset the following day with an excavator and a handful of trusted men to dig up what was hidden, and haul it away before Frank Keller ever knew he had company.

The dig started out by revealing pieces of metal debris densely scattered in the ground. It was made of an extremely lightweight metal alloy, clearly not a natural deposit of any kind. His hypothesis that it was all part of an even larger mass was confirmed after he excavated the entire area, unearthing what appeared to be vehicular wreckage. Carson had dug up a small, severely damaged vehicle comprised of a hull, tiny rocket engines, and not much else. The whole wreck gave off an intense heat, and he sweat heavily while near it. Inside the hull was empty except for the rear which held a viscous blue liquid that had leaked considerably onto the floor, presumably from either a fuel cell or power core, along with skeletal remains of what appeared to be a woman based on the remnants of clothing still covering the bones. Carson was awestruck by the find and took a moment to process the discovery as well as compose himself before directing his team, all of them as impressed by the find.

"No more digging. Don't touch anything inside. Load it on the flatbed and get it out of here."

Carson couldn't be sure but felt strongly that he had uncovered a flying vessel more advanced than anything he had ever seen, heard of, or read about. It was clear that the vehicle was causing the scorched markings on the ground above it, and he suspected the blue liquid inside was the cause. It was the only thing in the wreckage that seemed truly strange. The heat from the wreckage was hard to withstand for long, so Carson quickly looked around the vessel for any artifacts or items that might reveal clues about why it was buried in the middle of a cornfield in Denton. Finding a handful of translucent black crystals that had broken off from a larger piece lodged in the hull,

Carson grabbed them and left the site, instructing his workers to wrap up and deliver the discovery to his facility a few counties over. He walked back to his truck, which was parked a short distance from the field, and sat down at the wheel. He looked at the crystals he grabbed from the wreckage and pondered what he had just unearthed, but was interrupted by the feeling of cold metal against the side of his head.

"Carson."

Carson sat motionless, not even attempting to glance sideways at the shotgun pressing against him. "Hey, Frank. Out for a stroll tonight?"

"I found some small tread marks running through my field earlier this morning. You know anything about that?"

Carson raised his hands slowly. "Guilty, Frank." He feigned a laugh. "Guilty as charged."

"That was you I just saw digging up my field, then."

Carson swallowed nervously and cleared his throat. "Got me again, Frank. Can you lower your gun? Please?"

"No, I don't think so. We have a big problem now, Quest, and I'm not exactly sure how I am going to solve it. I don't want anyone to know about that field, or the spaceship you just found."

"Spaceship? What spaceship? That sounds like crazy talk, Frank. I can just drive away, and we can forget all about this." Despite his levity, Carson knew he was grasping at straws.

"I bet you could. What about all your friends though?"

"To be honest I don't like most of them, Frank, but you might. Why don't you go say hello, and show them your gun?"

Frank pulled the shotgun off Carson, cocked it, and then planted it firmly in his cheek.

"I think I'll just stay right here."

Carson stiffened. "What's your plan here, Frank? Are you gonna shoot everyone or just me?"

"Damn it, Carson! This isn't a game! Why did you dig up that ship?"

Carson turned his head slightly so that he could look Frank in the eyes. "Frank, I don't know. Curiosity got the best of me. Always does. You wanna tell me what the hell it is?"

"Get out of the truck."

"Frank—"

"—get out of the damn truck!"

"Alright. Alright. Take it easy. No need to get anxious." Carson exited the truck and stood face to face with Frank, who now pointed the barrel at his nose. "Let's talk. Just make sure your trigger finger doesn't get itchy, alright? You know, I had a suspicion it was an alien vessel. The stuff inside was just too unfamiliar. I'm assuming it crashed and you covered it over? Of course, it could have been anyone that did that, Frank. As far as I'm concerned you were never here tonight, and don't know anything about the ship. We can both just go our separate ways, and that's that."

"Not gonna happen." Frank firmed up his grip on his gun.

"Well, then what the hell, Frank? What are you gonna do? If you were going to shoot me you'd have done that by now. Do you realize what this discovery could lead to?"

"Calm down. You have no idea what you're dealing with nor any business dealing with it. That ship's not going anywhere."

"No, Frank, *you* don't know what you're dealing with. Do you know what would happen if the government found out what you've been hiding here? Frank, you might be in a world of trouble. I think you're going to need some help. I can't promise you anything right now, but if you lower that gun I'm sure we can—"

"—damn it, Carson!" Frank squeezed the trigger, but the safety was on.

Confused, Frank stood frozen for a moment.

Always a fast-acting opportunist, Carson reached forward and grabbed Frank's gun by the muzzle and wrenched it from his hands. He swung it around, slamming Frank's head with the stock. Frank fell to the ground. Carson switched off the safety and pointed the gun down at Frank.

"You can't stop a Quest."

He fired.

2

Elijah 'Eli' Quest arrived at the Interstellar Control Station orbiting Venus through a wormhole, which allowed him to bypass the months-long solar sailing ship cruise. The wormhole made the trip to the station, referred to as the "ICS" within his company, QuestCorp, as easy as driving to work, but for a man as busy as he was it was still more pain than pleasure. He liked running his empire from his office in Moon City, but the most recent project underway on the ICS demanded his presence. Communication delays between the station and his headquarters on the Moon prohibited him from managing the station in real time, and the experiment being tested was too important to leave in anyone else's care. The Venus operation was QuestCorp's second busiest site beyond Earth, overshadowed only by the company's headquarters in Moon City, which was the Mecca of Applied Sciences for the top scientific minds working at the company.

From the ICS, QuestCorp created and managed wormholes used to explore the corners of the universe previously only accessible through telescopes and observatories on the ground back on Earth. Through its explorations the company uncovered mysteries and harnessed resources almost daily that were, before QuestCorp's groundbreaking space program, beyond the scope of knowledge for even the smartest scientists studying the cosmos. Compared to Moon City, the control station was nothing glamourous, but the work done there was indispensable to the company's success.

The control station was managed by some of the most brilliant minds Earth had to offer; scientists who spent their days creating space-time interruptions and traveling to galaxies light-years away. Eli had personally recruited them for the purpose of developing and implementing interstellar travel, and QuestCorp profited immeasurably from the chain of discoveries that followed. The QuestCorp enterprise stretched from Mercury to Mars. It bound the solar system through its enterprise and was the sole intergalactic entrepreneurship.

As his shuttle exited the wormhole connecting Moon City and the control station, Eli's assistant, Nora Reinhard, engaged the autopilot to begin a docking sequence with the station.

"I'm still not used to it, Nora," Eli said, gazing out a portal at the planet below.

"Used to what?"

"Traveling through the wormhole."

"Would you rather take the Helios? A few months in a solar sailing ship might help you unwind."

"No."

"Well, then you'll get used to it, I guess." Nora was one of the few people who could speak candidly to Eli, and one of the few people who occasionally called him *Elijah*.

As the shuttle locked into the docking bay, Eli saw the scientists' operations vessels also docked at the station. He let out a heavy sigh. "I hope this is quick."

"It never is."

The shuttle doors opened, revealing a long corridor that led to the control station's large, round entrance door. The corridor had air but no gravity, and as Eli and Nora floated their way toward the station she nudged at his back with her foot.

"If you were anyone else I'd fire you," he said, glancing back at her over his shoulder.

"Go for it. I'm ready to go back to Earth anytime," she said while laughing.

She nudged him once more as they reached the control station doors. He looked back at her with a cold, prolonged stare that changed the mood instantly. Her face grew solemn. The doors opened, revealing the spinning interior of the control station. Centrifugal force was used to simulate gravity inside. The small platform where they were standing automatically moved them forward into the station. From it they stepped forward onto the rotating floor of the station, as if they were stepping onto an escalator.

The station itself was nothing more than a central control room with private quarters and escape pods lining the perimeter. Crammed into it were four scientists living out their dreams. They were amid technical discussions and test preparations when Eli and Nora walked in, but quickly shifted their focus. Some waved and exchanged some variation of pleasantries but stayed focused mainly on their test preparations. Elena Martinez, the station commander, came over to greet them.

"Eli. Nora. Welcome back to the ICS. It's going to be a hell of a day. How was your trip?"

Eli wasn't in the mood for pleasantries.

"Uncomfortable."

"Well, it beats the—"

"—beats a month in the Helios. I know. Thanks for the wormhole."

From a control desk, Edward, Elena's husband, shouted over. "Just a month? Unlikely. We are nowhere near optimal opposition right now. That wormhole just saved you a hell of a lot of time." Edward had a way of flaunting his intelligence, a quirk that bothered Eli.

Eli and Nora followed Elena into the control room and joined Edward at his station. "What do you have for me today, Edward?" Eli asked.

"It's ready, Eli. We've loaded the wormhole cache. We have a destination point for entry for every wormhole in the system, and no signs of destabilization." His enthusiasm was obvious.

Despite the impressiveness of Edward's work, Eli refused to show Edward enthusiasm. "Great. Now explain it so it makes sense. Like we talked about."

Edward stammered at Eli's curtness. Nora had a knack for getting him back on track though, by asking softer questions. "Edward, Eli keeps me in the dark with all of this stuff. What exactly are you doing here today?"

Engaged by the friendlier tone, Edward calmed down. "Hello, Nora. Good to see you. Right then, let me catch you up. So, you already know about wormholes. We've been setting them up, on demand, every time we needed one. Each time we choose a destination, we create a wormhole. Generally, the universe is an open form that spills out endlessly in every direction, yet we can pin any point within it as an actual place to go."

"Sure, you've been doing that for years," Nora said, politely trying to speed Edward along.

"Yes. We have. Now, imagine if we had been able to take all the wormholes we created over all those years, and save them like you would files on a computer. That's what we are doing here today. Or, well, what we have done already. Today we are going in to look around."

"Going in? I'm not following you," Nora asked.

"Right, so, here's the really cool part. We created a cache for the wormholes, then inserted it into four-dimensional space. Today we are going into that dimension to see how it's doing." The smile on Edward's face as he spoke was so large it looked almost menacing.

Nora's eyes widened as she listened to Edward explain the field operation. Eli, tired of Edward's roundabout way of getting to the point, stepped into the conversation to speed it along.

"How does it work, and be concise."

Edward cleared his throat and answered sheepishly. "Yes, um, yes. Well, okay, picture a piece of paper sitting on a desk. We'll say that the paper is the second dimension, and that it is resting against the desk, which in this discussion is the third dimension. Now, as the paper rests against the desk it is subject to whatever comes across the desk; wind, or clutter. It can be cut by scissors, or—"

"—I get it. Continue."

"Okay, so the paper can be influenced by three dimensional items on the desk surface, but if you take the paper and then place it inside a drawer of the desk, you've essentially moved the paper to a place where it can now rest inside the desk more securely, and still be easily accessed whenever it is needed."

Eli, annoyed by Edward's longwinded analogy, moved the conversation on to Arthur Chance, the station's resident contrarian and engineer. Eli had nicknamed him 'Last Chance', because he often got the last word in arguments within the group, even beating out Eli on occasion.

"Last Chance, does any of this matter?"

"No. In Edward's analogy, what he should be saying is that we are taking pages of paper and throwing them into the sea without having any idea of what lies beneath the water's surface. We aren't dealing with the second dimension. We're dealing with the fourth, and it's something we know absolutely nothing about. The fourth dimension can interact with our dimension in ways that we can't even perceive as another dimension."

"How?"

"Well, to use Edward's analogy, if the paper is the second dimension, we could stick a three-dimensional pencil through it, but only the cross section of the pencil would exist in the paper, or in the second dimension. The fourth dimension could theoretically do the same thing to us. The fourth dimension could cut us with scissors like we were paper, and we would have no idea why we were being cut, but would still suffer the cut. Edward seems to think that our dimension may already exist inside of the fourth dimension as a part of it, but there is no supporting evidence."

Edward chimed in to correct Arthur. "No, what I said was that the fourth dimension connects at every point of the third dimension as well as all the points around it."

Chance rolled his eyes. "Regardless, I built a containment structure for a large quantity of manipulated space-time, and we just bumped it from the known universe into one that we can't even comprehend because Edward thinks it's more conveniently accessible that way. Eli, you had us simultaneously pursue interstellar travel by wormhole and interdimensional mobilization through hyperspace because it couldn't be determined how the ship your father unearthed twenty years ago went interstellar. You know why we went with wormholes. The fourth dimension is just too damn hard to comprehend. We shouldn't be messing with it. I am good at what I do, but there is no way to predict structural capacity of the wormhole storage cache in an environment so foreign."

Edward butted in. "Arthur how can you say—"

"—Edward, Please! We lost people in there. People! They're out there floating around in a whole other damn dimension and we don't have a single good idea among us what to do about it. Now, you want to go in again? To look around? Eli, I know that you need portability, but creating this cache with a back door through the fourth dimension is just asking for trouble."

"It's groundbreaking science, Arthur, and we are sending a probe in anyway. No one needs to go in," Edward said, butting in again.

"It's dangerous, Edward. There has to be another way to bring it all with us."

Arthur and Edward exchanged scowls while Eli shook his head at both of them. "Thank you, Arthur," he said. "Your argument is noted. Edward, speaking to the facts about the third and fourth dimension, what exactly is your theory, and how does it work?"

Edward answered through a smug look on his face. "Eli, rather than connecting two points in the universe in a single space in a single moment as we do with wormholes each time we need one, we can have a wormhole created, stored, and ready for use within the fourth dimension. We can then travel to it from any point in our universe instantly through a hyperspace bridge into the fourth dimension. Essentially, we can take each wormhole from the top of the desk, and place them in the drawer together, where they will be tucked away indefinitely until we need them. And, we can open the drawer from anywhere. It's like quantum travel on speed dial."

"You've taken every connection we've made to our universe and placed them in the drawer. What if something is already in the drawer?" Eli asked.

Edward looked at Eli for a moment as if stunned or stumped by the question. "There is no way to know that."

The answer annoyed Eli. "Edward, I asked for a way to transport the control station and our wormhole generation capabilities so that it can come with us when we leave the solar system. I don't want to lose any of our current capabilities when we go to our new home. Would it have just been easier to build a new station on the other side beforehand?"

"Well, that's relative. I don't really know how to answer that. Easier than what?"

"Than messing around with this cache system you've created. If Chance says the fourth dimension is the wrong way to go, then why are we there at all? If it isn't right, walk away. Wormholes are fine. We don't need hyperspace."

Defensive, Edward went back at Eli. "Chance isn't always right. There is nothing wrong with what we are doing here today, and once we verify that everything is in order in the cache you'll be able to access the thing from the Moon if you wish. We've locked on individual destination points for entry into every wormhole we've stored. The system will automatically bring anyone who accesses it straight there from anywhere in the universe. The hyperspace bridge will only open to the destination point. I have simplified this process to the point where you won't even need us if you want to travel through a wormhole. I've done more than just make your system portable. I've made a physical file system in the fourth dimension of all the wormholes we travel through so that space exploration will be child's play and more readily available for the next generation of space travelers. This whole thing is for humanity, isn't it?"

Eli glared at Edward. Wading into a discussion of the ethics of the work was a fool's errand. From the moment he discovered the ship his father had stolen and murdered someone over, he wanted to use it for good. Reverse engineering it and then unpacking all its technology into new, usable QuestCorp technology that would lift the world up was enough of a penance paid for his father's crime.

"Edward, you are a problem solver, so just solve. I will decide how to use everything. Don't step out of line again."

"Sorry, Eli. I've just…we've…worked hard on this. It'll work. Trust me."

Eli was frustrated and leaning on the last of his patience. "We are all here, and I don't want to be here for nothing. Run the trial. In and out. I have other things to do today. Nora, run pre-launch on the shuttle. I want to be back on the Moon in an hour."

"Yes, sir."

Nora headed for the corridor that led to the docking bay while Edward stood silently, grinning at Eli.

"Get back to work, Edward."

"Right. Yes, sir." Edward scuttled back over to his workstation in the control room. While the scientists were finalizing the system check on the test probe, Eli walked over to speak with Chris Wu, another scientist working at the station. He was a true genius, a Master of Applied Science and reverse engineering. Wu had been quietly listening to the others bicker, which was typically his style.

"Wu, my darling, how are you?"

"Ready to rock, as always. It's good to see you. I was beginning to think you were afraid to leave your beloved Moon."

"Don't be dramatic. I'd leave the Moon any day to send my favorite scientist on a trip into another dimension."

Wu looked at Eli with confusion. "What do you mean? You don't want to send the probe?"

"No. You're going in. You unlocked every mystery on my father's ship. Without your discoveries, Edward's theories would have been a hundred years premature. This latest creation of his has me skeptical. I don't like the idea of placing interconnected portions of our universe inside another one. I trust your eyes, Wu. See this thing for yourself. If you tell me you see nothing wrong, then that's good enough for me. Okay?"

"Sure, no problem. I'll suit up." Wu left the control room as Eli addressed the others.

"Cancel the probe. We're sending Wu."

Looks of astonishment mixed with gasps of surprise came from the other members of the team. Everyone was used to Elena running field operations, and she was fanatical about keeping her people out of harm's way.

"Eli", Elena said, "I'm not sure about this. We haven't done any calculations for a human expedition."

"Just do it, Elena. I'm tired of waiting."

"Okay. You're the boss." Elena was fearless, and often charged smartly at problems and confrontations, but with Eli she chose sarcasm and passive aggressiveness to deal with him whenever he overstepped her role as station commander. "Flight suit on, Chris," she said, calling to Wu. "You're going in."

Wu walked back into the common area. "All done. I'm ready." He headed toward the docking bay. "I'll take the Sun Dog. Open the hyperspace bridge when I'm in view." The Sun Dog was a small craft, designed for speed and used for reconnaissance operations, and the first in the QuestCorp fleet to be built from the work Wu did on reverse engineering the vessel Eli's father had unearthed. As such, it was his favorite ship. Eli gave him the keys to it when he sent the team to Venus as a thank you.

"Once you see the bridge open, turn on your autopilot and punch in the destination point coordinates," Edward said.

"Okay, Ed."

"Enter your return coordinates while you are at it. Just in case," Elena added, a careful tone in her voice.

"Return trip. Got it. Anything else, Commander?"

"Be safe, Chris."

"Roger that. See you on the flip side." Wu hammed things up whenever he was excited, which was typically every mission. Eli appreciated the joviality that Wu brought to his work, but never mistook it for a lack of seriousness.

Wu headed down the corridor to the Sun Dog. Eli and the team watched him undock and maneuver the ship into position outside the control station windows. Once Wu was in position, Arthur opened a bridge into the fourth dimension; a tear in space large enough to slip the ship through into what looked like absolutely nothing at all. Once the bridge was open, Wu's autopilot took him through the opening, where he vanished. After he passed through there was no connection to him or his ship. It was as though he completely ceased to exist. Eli and the scientists stood silently, staring at the overhead screens that would normally display the flight data and vital statistics of the mission's spacecraft and personnel. Time seemed to stop. Eli broke the tension weighing on them all.

"How long will he be gone?"

Elena answered. "A few minutes. He knows what he should be looking for, and he'll know right away if he doesn't see it."

A few minutes came and went. The bridge remained open during the mission and Eli stared into it from the station's window. As he stared his eyes played tricks on him. He thought he saw movement like shadows in the dark, or a swirl of something that was disturbed along the edge of the bridge joining the two universes, but he dismissed it as his mind playing tricks. He worried that his rare rash judgment to send Wu into the unknown was turning out to be a huge mistake, and was genuinely worried for his friend's safety.

He was about to ask Elena what more they could do on their end to locate Wu when his ship slowly emerged across the bridge like a ghost ship listing in the night. Eerily, it crept back into the third dimension and then came to rest, motionless in front of them all, floating in the space just outside the control station. "What's going on? Where's Wu?" Eli demanded answers.

Elena began calling out orders. "Edward, get the ship's feeds back onscreen. Arthur, close the bridge. I want to see Wu. Get me the onboard cams. Get a visual now!" Edward and Arthur pounded at the keys at their control consoles, working quickly to get systems up and running. Slowly, data started popping up on the overhead screens; feeds from the Sun Dog. The ship's system diagnostics scrolled on one screen while another showed video of the hyperspace bridge closing in on itself. Arthur had shut it down. The onboard cams started to populate the remaining empty screens overhead in the control room. A video feed of Wu came up. He appeared unconscious. Elena called to him through the intercom.

"Wu, are you okay? Respond. Wu, respond, this is Elena."

There was no response. Elena and her team brought his ship into dock using the autopilot and retrieved him. He was alive, breathing ever so faintly, with a faint pulse. Eli was horrified.

"Put him on my shuttle with Nora and open a wormhole to the Moon."

"Yes, sir. What do you want us to do about the cache?" Elena asked.

"Shut it down. Shut everything down and come back to the Moon in the Helios. I'll send it to you as soon as I return to Moon City. I don't want any of you opening any more wormholes and stay the hell away from the fourth dimension. Run diagnostics. Find out what happened. I don't want another incident. Arthur, you are in charge. Get it done."

"Yes, sir."

"Edward, I want to see you as soon as you get to Moon City."

Eli shut the door, the shuttle undocked, and then headed through the wormhole back to the Moon.

3

Savior was on a rescue mission in a war-torn neighborhood in the middle eastern city of Ba 'albek. As he searched for refugees from the tops of crumbling rooftops and through winding corridors littered with rubble, it wasn't long before he found a group of people desperately trying to escape the bloody civil war. Amid the aging alleyways, this small band of people scrambled along, desperate to escape the legions of rebel fighters and royal armed forces that attacked anything that moved in the broad day warzone.

Savior came upon the refugees not as the invincible hero of the world he was known to be, but as a stranger dressed in long brown robes and wearing a keffiyeh that draped down and covered his face except for his sharp-blue eyes. He appeared before them as if from nowhere, standing tall and broad, and in broken language and a foreign tone, told them to follow him. They followed. The group slowly and silently moved in single file along the backstreets and alleys of their city, leaving home behind for a chance at peace in some place new. The sounds of war surrounded them: machine gun fire, artillery shell explosions, military orders yelled to soldiers, bystanders' screams of agony. The roar and hum of heavy machinery on the move nearby was heard and felt by all as it shook the ground. As they travelled, frightened grandmothers consoled grandchildren, and mothers and fathers silenced the cries of their children by covering their mouths and eyes. Through the constant sounds of violence, Savior reacted to each noise, pausing, listening, looking back and forth, and then gesturing to the refugees to duck, hide, or run, depending on the threat of danger. He covertly led the group on an escape route through a dynamic battlefield where armies engaged one another in pockets throughout the city. The sweltering heat of the day simmered as the refugees put one foot in front of the other in their mad dash to escape. Death or escape were the only options for these uprooted people, but Savior refused to accept death as an option. If it meant carrying them all one by one, he would see these people freed from the warzone threatening to eat them whole. It was his way. Without knowing who the people were, he worked hard to save them. In a crude attempt at speaking their language, he tried to motivate the people.

"iibqa' qidmayk tataharak. 'anaha tahmil hayatak' .alyawma. la tade lahum yaetaqidun khilaf dhalik."

The words brought a calm focus amid the clamor, as though everyone realized that they were saving their lives simply by running for them.

Savior brought them to a high wall at the end of a narrow corridor. He signaled for the refugees to stop, then urged them to stay low and hidden. He stared at the wall briefly, looking left and right along its lengths as if to reason out which way was safest, shortest, or the most realistic way to proceed. It was an old city, and not all walls and streets made sense. Of greater concern to him were the heavy tanks he heard rolling on the other side of the wall and the battalion of troops marching alongside them. Savior looked back from the wall at the people. He gestured to them with his large, steady hand to stay put, and within a small field of wild electricity that spontaneously generated around his body, he disappeared into thin air, reappearing instantly on the other side of the wall.

Machine gunfire rattled off immediately, and a barrage of bullets needled him with relentless frequency. They struck him viciously, but bounced away, piercing his robes but nothing else. Unaffected by the spray of bullets, he was briefly knocked off balance by additional hand grenades and gunfire shot at him from behind. Commands and battle cries then rang out as even more explosions shook the ground around him. Dust flew up and darkened the sky, making it impossible to see anything even just inches away. Only a wall of ancient bricks stood between this chaotic battle and the crowd of refugees he was leading to safety.

The bullets and bombs did not cease. Savior was the only man on Earth that could stand alone against an entire army, but he stayed humble in the heat of battle. He wanted to clear the path of danger but didn't want to take lives if they could be spared. He struck the fighters just hard enough to render them unconscious. He grabbed machine guns and snapped them in half with his hands, and teleported tanks into the sky, letting gravity smash them and render them immobile. Bombs continued to go off near him and set him off his course, but he regained his footing each time and was on the attack before the blasts cleared.

In the mayhem of the battle a tank round blasted Savior, knocking him hard into the wall, which caused a tremendous explosion. The wall partially collapsed, and dust and debris scattered everywhere. It was difficult to see through the dust cloud, but Savior saw the refugees scramble every which way, spared from the explosion but now exposed to the fighting. The gunfire and explosions from behind stopped. The dust began to settle, and the shapes of stones, piles of rock, and jagged blocks of a wall blown apart began to reemerge. Sunlight shining in from the hole in the wall shone down on Savior, who was partially covered by debris. In the illuminated dust-filled air, he rose. His body armor, black tactical gear that had become symbolic of the hero, was visible underneath his now tattered robes. He passed back through the hole in the wall and reengaged his enemy, who responded with more bullets and grenades. Savior fought back, hurting the fighters and destroying weapons. With confused orders to run or retreat filling the air, the fighting ended just as quickly as it began. Savior returned through the wall, his robes now scraps of cloth, his face now uncovered. He was completely unharmed. The refugees gathered, staring in total disbelief at the hero who stood before them.

"'ant alan amin," he said before electrifying and then disappearing.

4

Eli was flying over the Moon's landscape in an aerial transport drone. The vehicle was nearing the end of its trial phase and was about to be made available to his employees in Moon City as a replacement for the company's lunar rovers. The drone moved effortlessly over the Moon's surface, flying ten feet above the ground on a course programmed by a GPS system QuestCorp had developed specifically for the Moon. As the drone hovered along on its course, Eli looked out the window at the city he'd built. His company was about to change the world, and shortly he'd be sharing the details in a press conference. He had made QuestCorp thrive in outer space, and the view of the boundless emptiness beyond the Moon's horizon exemplified the freedom his company had found there.

QuestCorp was a far-reaching enterprise, tapping pockets all over the universe full of wonderful new elements and minerals, as well as stocks of precious metals and gems already valued on Earth. It was as though Eli, through his intergalactic endeavors, had become an astral jeweler that peddled the stars, dealing out pieces of the cosmos from his city on the Moon. Moon City was a first-of-its-kind lunar base, built to support the full array of the company's cosmic reach. It was a research laboratory, factory, and an operational marvel. It was also the corporate headquarters for all of Eli's business arms back on Earth. Every aspect of QuestCorp was tied to Moon City, yet the base itself was virtually autonomous. Fuel, food, and material needs were created onsite, and other than personnel transportation and data transmissions, the lunar base existed in isolation. For Eli, the Moon could not have been a better place to establish an independent stronghold. This test drive in the drone gave him the chance to take in the visual of his booming empire.

The Moon was a pristine, uninhabited, barren landscape littered with craters and sharp-edged ridges. The view in all directions was crystal clear, revealing an undisturbed state of beauty save for the sparse rover tracks. The beauty of the landscape's desolateness aside, there was no better place to establish his headquarters. Moon City sprawled along the lunar landscape. Had it been built on Earth there would have been major gravitational challenges to its architectural design as well as zoning regulations because if its acres of mass, not to mention finding enough open space to accommodate the spread. Operating on the Moon also kept any forms of control hundreds of thousands of miles away; no government on Earth could claim ownership of the Moon or attempt to govern it. It was a freedom for Eli that, despite all his wealth, was simply unaffordable on Earth.

A warning alert sounded from the drone's control panel: *"Battery capacity is at fifty percent. Rerouting to Moon City."*

Eli scowled, then called into the base from the comm. "Nora, I'm on my way back in. What is the ETA on the Helios?"

Nora answered back immediately: *"It's making final approach."*

The Helios was carrying his crew of scientists from the ICS, completing a three-month round trip to retrieve them. Eli wanted Edward on hand for questions at the press conference and had timed it to the solar sailing ship's arrival. The arrival of the scientists meant there was little time before the press conference where he would map out his vision of the future. As the drone returned to base, Eli observed the Helios' approach.

A crowd of journalists was moments away from landing on the Moon as well; the first guests ever to set foot in Moon City. They were flying in on a shuttle designed and built by QuestCorp that could function as either cargo ship or passenger shuttle, and once they landed they would be ushered into a press room where Eli would address them. While the drone was docking, he pulled some notes from a pocket in his flight suit and glanced at them, rehearsing what he planned to say in his address. He was a confident man, but the scope of what he was about to unveil to the journalists, and the world, was greater than anything he had ever undertaken. Even though Eli had already commandeered the inner planets of the solar system, he was about to make his play for Earth.

As he rehearsed his speech, the landing bay pressurized, and Nora entered. Nearing Eli's drone, she shouted to him. "They're here. Both ships have arrived."

Looking out past the billions of stars dotting the backdrop of outer space one last time, Eli closed his eyes, letting his breath out slowly in a moment of mediation before exiting the vehicle. "Look out there, Nora. Have you ever seen anything more wondrous?"

"Yeah. Every day on Earth. I want to go home."

Eli scowled and then turned to face Nora. "How is Wu today?"

"No change."

"Any new theories from the medical staff?

"No. They want to speak to his family."

"Get the press to their seats. Let me know when they are ready. Retrieve Edward from the Helios and tell him to head into the press room. And tell the engineers they have a problem with the battery on the drone. It isn't holding its charge."

"Yes, sir."

Nora left to greet and prepare the journalists. Eli, alone in the landing bay, closed his eyes once more, briefly held his hand to his mouth, and then whispered aloud, "It's time." He opened his eyes, and as he entered the corridors of Moon City to head to the pressroom he resumed his hard-nosed confidence.

As he walked up to the lectern in the pressroom the crowd of journalists he had invited were filing in, yet were distracted by the up-close view of the lunar landscape. He watched as they took notes and photos of what he agreed was an astonishing view.

"It's quite a view," he said, speaking into the microphone at the lectern. The journalists reacted to Eli with a collective, startled jerk followed by a rough and clumsy self-ushering to the pressroom seats, which turned just as quickly into a barrage of questions.

"Please, everyone, save your questions. I promise they will all be answered before you go home." The crowd laughed nervously, but settled in. "First, let me thank you for making the flight here. Our passenger program is new, but since you arrived here safely without any issues during the long flight, I trust you will write kindly about the experience once you've returned to Earth. How weird is *that* to say?" More laughs. "Ladies and gentlemen, welcome to the Hydrogen Age. It is with tremendous pride and humility that I announce to you a revolution, or evolution, if you will, of the care and capabilities of our species. The time has finally come when we can look beyond the limitations of our home to see the bright future of mankind. My company, QuestCorp, has gone beyond the limits of Earth in order to secure peace and prosperity never before seen or experienced; one that can never be exhausted or taken away. What will start after we conclude here today is a project we refer to in Moon City as the Demeter Initiative. What this project has done and what it has yet to do will simply blow your minds. Outside those windows is just a very small piece of a complicated and vast resource acquisition program entering its eleventh year of operation. For over a decade now, folks here on the Moon, and elsewhere in the solar system, have been harvesting hydrogen from the Sun. That's right, the Sun; the burning ball of unlimited power at the heart of our solar system and the root of so much of what we are thankful for on Earth. We are collecting its energy in a very complicated way and storing it here on the Moon for processing before shipping it to Earth as a new fuel source ready to do some good. We will hand you literature on all of that for the flight home. This fuel can be used as an energy utility and for food production for all the people of Earth. It's true; in fact, we're already doing it here on the Moon. QuestCorp is proud to announce that through our groundbreaking innovations we have brought the world the final solution to all its fundamental needs, and with these needs met, our vision will usher in a new and final peace. Our science has already developed a variety of platforms, and we will be partnering with corporations and governments all over the world to share our knowledge.

The aim of our partnerships is to secure power and sustenance to all people of Earth and to eliminate conflicts driven by energy needs as well as various other land-based issues. By providing this we will unlock the doors to a better future for all of mankind, which will allow us to develop our collective greatness. There is nothing to limit us now. Questions?"

The pressroom erupted. Questions spilled from every mouth in the room in one audible dump, making any chance at comprehending a single word impossible. In the raucous disorder, Eli called on a reporter for a question.

"Where is Emilia? Emilia Trust, what questions does the *News Today's* senior reporter have for me?"

Emilia was one of the louder voices in journalism, so the crowd settled as Emilia asked her question.

"Mister Quest, thank you. How are you harvesting hydrogen from a source as far away as the Sun? And, in doing so, can you verify your claim that you will be able to mass produce products from the harvested hydrogen?"

"Miss Trust, that's two questions. Let me just reiterate to everyone that we are going to send you home with binders of information on how it all works, plus, we have our lead scientist here to meet with you all today to discuss the science of things as well. To quickly address your questions though, you are right. We can't go to the Sun and scoop out hydrogen. An operation like that just didn't add up. So, we bring the Sun to us. Our lead scientist, Doctor Edward Martinez, along with a league of the very best scientists and engineers, developed an ingenious method for harvesting hydrogen. It's called Siren, and it is an artificially intelligent orbital spacecraft designed to capture hydrogen isotopes from the sun and pass them along to transport vessels in space. From a position just beyond Venus, it operates a high-powered dual laser with specific wavelengths that are directed at the Sun, which also carry a very particular set of proton and electron charges along its beams. The charges are unique and developed specifically by Doctor Martinez and his team to interact with the Sun's magnetic field, and the hydrogen as well. A charge on the first laser attracts hydrogen at and near the Sun's surface, pulling it away along the beam. Once the hydrogen is drawn to the beam, a second charge of negative electrons is then sent out along the second laser, attracting the newly protonic charged hydrogen toward the negative charge on the laser and back to Siren. Hence, a *hydrogen stream* is created. Once the hydrogen reaches the laser beam's origin at Siren, it is loaded into massive drone transport ships that then travel by solar sail to here, Earth's Moon, where the hydrogen is unloaded into the large, secure storage facilities you can all see through those windows.

Now, it took a lot to get the stream flowing, but we've had a continuous flow for nearly five years with no signs of it stopping. Miss Trust, we have five years' worth of harvested hydrogen already processed in reserve tanks here in Moon City, and we can deliver it to Earth safely today using two special shuttles we have designed and built here on the Moon, one of which brought you here. We are currently building two more upgraded shuttles, and plan to have them in operation within six months of each other starting six months from now. Estimates predict that it will take twenty years to deplete what we have harvested in the last five, and we will be expanding our harvesting capability, storage facilities, and distribution network continually within that timeframe. Miss Trust, QuestCorp would not do it if it couldn't be done, and we specialize in finding ways to do all the things that can't be done. Next question. Tobias?"

"Mister Quest, what is the tech you have developed for the energy capability piece, and will people want to eat this *food* that you've created?"

A tech question from a tech blogger. "Another twofer. Toby, I am forever amazed by what some people will eat, but at the end of the day, food is food. We need it, and some places need it more than others. I am happy to offer a meal wherever a meal is in need. As for energy capability, we are keeping things simple. Our innovative fuel cells and power cores will be able to power anything from cars to industrial machinery to homes to hospitals to skyscrapers. Imagine no more power grid; power generation can now be done on site where and when it is needed. There is considerably less waste and impact on the environment, less inconveniences to users, and the ability to go anywhere because we can refuel them with drones. Any other questions, Toby?"

"Just one. Are these power cores stable and safe?"

"They are safe as can be. They actually power our robotics as well as our entire operation here on the Moon. The options for use are limitless."

Eli was about to call on another question from the reporters when Nora entered the room, quickly walked up to him at the lectern, and then whispered something into his ear. A startled look followed by one of aggravation came and went from his face. After a glance at the reporters in the pressroom, he addressed them briefly. "Thank you everyone for coming out. I am afraid I will have to end this early, but I would like to ask Edward Martinez, our lead scientist, to take over your questions.

Please, enjoy your stay, and have a safe flight home. Thank you."

As Eli left the lectern the reporters erupted with a thunderous storm of questions. As he neared the exit, Edward Martinez greeted everyone from the lectern. "Hello. Please settle. Please settle. My name is Edward. I'm sorry I'm not Eli, but I am more than happy to answer your questions. Before we start I'll tell you a little about myself. I'm a Theoretical Physicist from Cambridge. I've led the teams here at QuestCorp responsible for the Demeter Initiative for sixteen years, and I've lived here on the Moon or in orbit above Venus for the last five. I can answer anything you might want to ask about the project, from how and when it started to where it is going. So, who'd like to go first?"

Questions poured from every mouth in the room. Edward gulped nervously, and then called on a reporter.

5

Eli walked into his office to the sight of his father, Carson, sitting in a wheelchair behind the desk looking out the office windows at the Moon. He was drinking a glass of Eli's Macallan Sherrywood 40-year aged single malt scotch. He looked ancient and ailed, but Eli was surprised to see him in Moon City no matter the condition. Eli sat down in a chair on the visitor's side of his desk. "I thought you were serving a life sentence. How much did you pay the warden for an early release?"

Carson turned his wheelchair to face Eli. "Elijah, my son. Good to see you too. I was just listening in on your little press conference. My, how you've changed in twenty years. Looking a little gray, eh boy?"

"Cut the shit, Dad. Why are you here?"

"All business. You never change, do you? Since you're asking, they didn't let me out, son. I broke out. Can you imagine? A guy my age. I had some help, obviously. Needed someone to push this damn chair, but I still think it's a pretty unbelievable feat to have pulled off. Anyway, I needed somewhere to go, so I thought, *why not visit the boy?* I don't know what kind of show you're running up here, but I'm guessing there isn't all that much as far as law enforcement is concerned. I hope you don't mind."

"You are the last person I would ever want to see; here or anywhere. I'm putting you on a shuttle back to Earth. It leaves in a few hours. Enjoy what little time you have left as a free man."

Carson scoffed in a playful way. "Typical. Just what I expected from you, Elijah. My disappointment in you will never be abated, it seems. You're too predictable. Always have been. It's so boring."

"I've given you more time than you deserve. Don't push your luck."

A scowl came over Carson's face as he firmly placed his scotch down on Eli's desk, splashing a little onto a computer keyboard. "Don't you lecture me about pushing. If I push you it's just pushing back! You practically pushed me into prison after that misunderstanding with Keller."

"It wasn't a misunderstanding. It was a murder."

"It was self-defense! The crazy old man had a gun to my head. What was I supposed to do?"

"You were stealing from his farm."

"Yeah, maybe. I prefer to think of it as advancing science for humanity. Besides, you stole it from me afterward. What does that say about you?"

"I didn't shoot someone in the face. And I only discovered what you dug up when I took over GroQuest for you."

"Took over? You shut it down."

"I restructured it."

"You took its name away! It was a multi-million-dollar company. Now it's in some corner behind all your robotics and medical research and mining. And, now this." Carson gestured toward the window.

Eli smirked, amused by his father's exacerbation. "Is that why you're here, Dad? You wanted to get a look at all my success? Take another look out that window. Do you know how many of those stars we've visited? Digging in the dirt suited you. But I prefer flying through the stars with my multi-*billion*-dollar company."

"You're a bastard."

"That says more about you than it does about me."

"I'm your father, damn it!"

"You're a convict, and a murderer. I don't see you as anything else."

"Eli. Enough. I don't want this. I don't want to do this with you. We've already done enough of this. A damn lifetime of bickering. After twenty years, I just want to talk."

Eli crossed his arms and looked sternly at his father. "About what?"

Carson looked at Eli long enough for Eli to stare back into his eyes. He could finally see the root of the pain and fear that was now driving his father's actions. "I'm dying, Eli. It's incurable."

"I'm sorry, Dad."

"Thank you, son. It means a lot to me to hear you say that. I know I was hard on you your whole life, but you turned out alright. I can't believe my boy built a city on the Moon. I'm proud of you. I mean that."

"You're being dramatic."

"I just can't help but wonder if any of your success ever would have happened if it wasn't for me finding the spaceship that you stole from me."

"Ah. There it is. This is about you."

"Oh, shut up. I just want to know what it is. You must have studied it."

They stared at each other, and the sadness in Carson's eyes was genuine. Eli could see an old, tired, and broken man. He took pity.

"Yes. The ship you discovered was the start of everything."

"Ha! I knew it! Tell me everything, even if it takes until I die."

"Enough of the dramatics. You found a space ship from another world. It was mostly destroyed, but there were some retrievable computer systems and some pieces of technology that survived the crash. It took a lot to unlock the information, but what little we got gave us a tremendous leap in artificial intelligence, data processing, and interstellar travel."

Carson writhed with excitement in his chair. "What about the bones?"

"Not human. Very similar anatomically but very different structurally. They match nothing on Earth. She was a female."

"An alien?"

"Definitely not a human."

Carson sat back in his chair, grinning at the ceiling, with a look of vindication on his face. "Amazing. Thank you. I knew it was a true discovery the moment I saw it. Worth the twenty years and more."

"Worth the life you took?"

"What else did you learn?"

Eli grimaced, and then decided to answer the question. "From the ship, plenty. We learned a lot from the crystals too. Those crystals that you found turned out to be a vicious little discovery. We tried to unlock their mysteries through testing how they interacted with different items from the ship."

"What did you find?"

"They didn't react with the ship or any of the technology at all. They did react to the remains, however. Or, rather, the bones reacted to them."

"Fascinating."

"More like gruesome. When we placed the crystals and the remains together it stimulated a reaction in the bones that caused them to act in a parasitic way. At first, they rapidly decayed. As a countermeasure, they tried to bond and absorb energy from any organic material nearby. It was an accidental discovery. An unfortunate researcher was severely injured during the experiment. When we studied the bones more closely we learned that their cellular structure was more closely related to plant cells than animal cells. The crystals seemed to weaken the bone's cell structures, which triggered a regenerative instinct in the life form. Those are just observations and theory though. We really can't identify the relationship between the two. The crystals' composition is too foreign to any of the elements we know."

"Remarkable. What else?"

"She wasn't alone."

"No?"

Eli walked around to his desk drawers and pulled out another crystal, clear like a diamond and about the size of a fist. "The crystals you took were fragments contaminated by radioactive spillage from the ship's power core. This one, however, is different. This one is a computer. Although we are still trying to understand how it stores data, we have been able to access everything in it. It belonged to a scientist from another planet. We found a lot of data about his home world on it along with a lot of video footage. The last entry is of him and his wife fleeing their world as it disintegrated. She was pregnant. We think the remains in the ship were hers. But there was no evidence of any offspring."

"A child? On Earth!?"

"There is no record of a birth in the crystal, but we investigated. Your discovery did a lot of things, Dad, one of which was reveal the hidden truth behind Savior."

"Savior? The 'Hero of Mankind' is an alien? Of course. It makes sense. How long have you known?"

"Since before he was called Savior."

"Does he know that you know?"

"No. And, he more than likely doesn't know *what* I know, either."

"So, what are you going to do?"

"He isn't part of my plans. Frankly, neither are you. I am sorry that you are ill. I hope all this information gives you comfort in your final days. My assistant is going to escort you to the shuttle, and then back to prison. She needs to get out of town for a while anyhow."

"Thank you, Eli. It means a lot that you told me all of this."

Eli looked at his father briefly. He was no reflection of the man he once was, and no one Eli felt he needed to care for anymore. Carson was powerless, and a man of no means. Eli was glad to give a dying man a bit of peace but didn't have the time to invest in much else with him.

"You're welcome. Goodbye."

Eli left his father with the best view of the stars he would ever see. He called for Nora.

"Return my father to prison. He mentioned having some help to get here. Have the city searched for his accomplice and return him as well if he is here. Spend some time on Earth, if you wish. And fire the pilots that brought him here."

He didn't stop walking as he spoke to her, nor did he look back as he left.

6

Emilia Trust was sitting at a table alone in a Moon City cafeteria, near windows that overlooked the lunar landscape. She was preparing for an interview by reviewing notes she had taken at the press conference, though anxiously looked forward to going home. A server approached.

"Can I get you something to drink while you wait for Doctor Martinez, Miss Trust?"

"Yes, thanks. Balvenie neat. Hey, are there windows in every room in this place?"

"What good would living on the Moon be if you couldn't see any of it? I'll be right back with your drink."

Emilia looked out the window. Off in the distance there were elevations that reminded her of the mountains back home. She was certainly impressed by the Moon, but to her it was nothing compared to Earth. It looked nice, but that was about it. Plus, there weren't any stories to chase. She had come to the Moon for the press conference only after receiving a guarantee from Eli Quest that she would have the first exclusive interview with him after he made his announcement. She had a tip on a story she wanted to call him out on and was irritated that she had been pushed off onto Edward Martinez instead.

After Martinez took over the press conference, he hadn't impressed her. With a fair amount of time before the next shuttle flight back to Earth, she hoped he might give her something unique left out of the press conference.

"Here you are, Miss Trust," the server said as she delivered her scotch.

"Thank you."

"You're welcome. If you need anything else, my name is Karen. Doctor Martinez will be here shortly," Karen said while pointing to a corridor that entered the cafeteria.

"Thank you, Karen. I'm all set."

The server went off to her other tables, and Emilia looked over to where she had pointed and saw Edward already walking toward her. He smiled and waved at her awkwardly. He joined her at the table and shook her hand as he sat down across from her. He already had a drink.

"Hello, Miss Trust. Nice to meet you. I'm a big fan of your newspaper."

"Please, call me Emilia. Are you from Chicago?"

"No, no I'm from Bibury originally. England."

"I'm sorry, I've never heard of it."

"It's a beautiful place. Charming buildings. Lots of green. Quite lovely if that's your sort of thing. About as opposite of here as you could possibly get. Chicago too, I'm sure."

"Well, I didn't know we circulated in Bibury. I'll have to add it to my vacation list; it sounds lovely. Thank you for meeting with me, Doctor. You run a very impressive show up here."

"Please, call me Edward. And, thank you. This place is a dream come true for me."

"Really? A base on the Moon is your dream come true?" Emilia wasted no time digging in.

"Well, not in that sense, no. What we do here. Sorry."

"Not at all. QuestCorp really has exploded up here, that's for sure. I mean, the Demeter Initiative is a big deal. Unlimited power for the entire world, and food too? How does *that* work exactly?"

"Do you want the quick answer or the long one?"

"There isn't another shuttle for hours, but if you go into too much detail my eyes will glaze over."

Edward laughed. "Right then, the short answer. Okay. So, just about everything humans eat is made from hydrocarbons; molecules that make up pretty much all the vegetables and animals that we eat."

"Okay."

"Well, what we have done is synthesize hydrocarbons in order to manufacture that food. Simply put, we use Siren to harvest hydrogen atoms from the Sun, specific ones called tritium, which hang about in the cosmic rays surrounding the Sun, and in a controlled fission reaction we—"

Emilia's eyes widened. "—fission? Like, the bomb?"

"Well, yes, but a controlled reaction, and on a small and repetitive scale. We use the fission reaction to blow apart the tritium isotopes, separating the protons, neutrons, and electrons which we then use as building blocks to build carbon atoms."

"Which you use to make food." Emilia sipped on her drink.

Edward smiled. "Almost. We bond the new carbon atoms with other hydrogen isotopes to make hydrocarbons, which are used to make the food. We also collect the heat energy released from the fission reactions with tungsten to use as a power source during the process and recycle the leftover neutrons to bombard more tritium before they decay. It's a remarkably efficient process. We actually use a similar process to build synthetic vitamins and minerals to add to the hydrogen-based food, making it as nutritious as conventional food."

"You lost me, Edward. But, that sounds like really amazing stuff. You are doing some smart things up here. And all that is safe?"

"Entirely. We engineered a one-of-a-kind facility where we process the reactions. It's like nothing on Earth."

"Impressive. Tell me more."

Edward grinned. "That's about all I can say on that. To be honest, I didn't have much of a hand in the food project other than overseeing the development of Siren."

"But in the press conference you said you run Demeter."

"Yes, that's true, but my real contribution is more on the interstellar side of things. It's sort of the backdrop of everything we've been able to accomplish."

"So, you are the man behind the curtain."

Edward laughed. "No, no. Eli is the man behind the curtain. And, in front of it. He's everywhere, really. I just had a lot of good ideas and he believed in them."

"And now all of this."

"Yes. Now all of this. That's right."

"I can't let you off the hook since you brought it up. What are you doing with interstellar? I heard that was over."

Edward was caught off guard. "Where did you hear that?"

"Sources."

Edward looked at Emilia for a moment, as if to appreciate her cunning or to solve her like a puzzle. "Would you like to take a walk, Miss Trust? A tour?"

"Sure, Edward. I would love a tour." Emilia feigned interest. She could see Edward dodging the question from a mile away but thought that he was certainly the type who would let something slip out if given the chance to keep talking. Before they left the cafeteria, she ordered another round of drinks for them, which they took on the tour.

Despite her lack of interest, the tour was still impressive. There was a full array of luxuries for employees in the many dormitories that housed the huge staff on the Moon: domed recreation fields for sports activities, lunar touring rovers driven by automated guidance systems, a livestock farm, and fishing at a communal hydroponic farm. The views were breathtaking everywhere. From an operations perspective, the Moon base was a beehive of activity. There were desks and workstations everywhere, and each one was stationed with people intensely monitoring systems on multiple screens, talking on headsets, typing on keyboards, and in one or two cases, scratching their heads in bewilderment. People were zipping around from one desk to another working on several tasks at once, and the whole station buzzed with numerous conversations that never stopped. It was exactly what Emilia had expected to see in a place called Moon City. As Edward lead her through the facilities, he explained them as if reading from long and boring scripts. Occasionally, she would ask a question to probe Edward and lead him into a conversation that might be worthwhile, but Edward just continued with the tour.

Growing tired of the game, Emilia became a bit more direct with Edward. She pointed out a window that faced the giant ten-story storage tanks of hydrogen. "What are the consequences of all of this, Edward? There is a downside to everything. What are you leaving us in the dark about?"

"I'm sorry, Emilia, what do you mean?"

"I mean you're conducting routine fission operations here on the Moon; blasting apart atoms, making all these spare parts, releasing all this energy. What about radiation? What about negative effects? And, what about the Sun? How much hydrogen can you take before it's too much?"

Edward chuckled a little. "All of those questions are good questions, and the answers to them really are why we are here on the Moon. But, to answer your last question first, you needn't worry about hurting the Sun. It contains ninety-nine percent of the solar system's mass. I doubt there is anything we could do to hurt it. As far as negative effects of our operations, hosting our operations here on the Moon negates those effects for everyone on Earth. With energy production, there is always waste, so that's true for us here too. There is radioactive decay even though we are pretty good at minimizing it. There are consequences to how we manipulate hydrogen, but we do all that stuff here on the Moon so that it never is a problem back on Earth. What we ship to Earth is all clean, processed product; material that has been made ready for use as fuel and for food production. It's all refined and environmentally safe. We keep what's bad here on the Moon until we can ship it to Venus on drone ships, where it is then staged for return to the Sun. It's the most Earth-friendly fuel there has ever been. Energy production can cease entirely on Earth, and the planet can begin to restore itself, climate-wise, et cetera."

"You're not worried about affecting the environment here on the Moon?"

"No. There is no environment here, and the alternative is to affect the environment on Earth. Earth can't handle much more of that, in my opinion. It was never a goal of mine, but I'm happy to be doing my part to help save the Earth."

Emilia walked away from the conversation. There were enough journalists covering environmental issues and scientists working to save the environment. She decided to pull her wildcard. Her sources told her about a robotic force being built by QuestCorp, but she hadn't been able to confirm its existence.

"Edward, is S.W.A.R.M. powered by the Sun too?"

"Yes, it is. Everything we do runs off our power source."

Edward had taken the bait without realizing it, so Emilia pressed on. "Did you develop S.W.A.R.M.?"

"No, I'm not much of an engineer. S.W.A.R.M. is a project of Eli's. He controls it. He keeps it all very close to his chest. He developed it to help people in crises like natural disasters or people experiencing famine due to drought and such. It's remarkable, really."

"How does it work?"

"It's an AI. It's semi-autonomous. Eli runs it. It's going to serve as the workforce on Earth for the Demeter Initiative."

"And it's safe?"

"Totally."

"So, what exactly do you do, Edward? If the food and the harvesting and the S.W.A.R.M. are all part of the Demeter Initiative, but you have nothing to do with any of it, what do you do? I just want to have all the facts right. No offense."

Edward, indeed looking slightly offended, answered the question. "No, no. Of course. I oversee the teams who work on all these things even though I am not directly involved. The Demeter Initiative is the most recent iteration of our work over the last decade and a half. My main contribution is on our interstellar program. I don't mean to brag, but I invented the functional wormhole, among other things."

"So, what's next in interstellar, Edward?"

"Interstellar isn't something we talk about all that much. The wormhole is a pretty sensitive project."

"What can you tell me about it?"

"Not much, I'm afraid. It is what it sounds like. Using it, we travel to different parts of the universe by manipulating space-time."

"To go where? To do what?"

"Initially, the idea was to survey, do some exploratory mining, and a lot of mapping."

"I remember the press release from back when it began trials. Is that all?"

"All I can tell you."

Regardless, Emilia had what she wanted; Martinez confirmed S.W.A.R.M., and then some. "Okay, well thank you, Edward. I'm sure there is a story in there somewhere."

"Right, well, glad I could give you something to make your trip worthwhile. Eli is sorry he had to cancel."

"I'm sure he is. Just one more question, Edward, if you don't mind."

"Of course."

"What is QuestCorp's endgame? What is it planning with all this stuff?"

"I'm sorry, Emilia. I think that's a question you really should save for Eli. If you'll excuse me, I must meet my wife for dinner. Can you find your way back?"

"Yes. Thank you."

"Cheers."

Emilia watched Edward as he walked away. S.W.A.R.M. was going to be a huge story, and she was going to need a strategy for putting the story out. She wanted to get back to Earth right away to meet with her editor-in-chief, and to think through the story she just cracked open: QuestCorp had developed a way to travel anywhere in the universe, invented a way to harvest unlimited power, *and* created a robot workforce controlled by just one man. There would be major blowback for a story like that.

7

Nora and Carson flew back to Earth in the same shuttle as all the reporters from the press conference. She was carrying out Eli's order to return his father to prison, which was an order she was more than happy to carry out. Carson Quest was the vilest man she had ever met. Unfortunately, one of her roles as Eli's assistant had been to manage Carson, because Eli refused to deal with him. So, over the years she had visited him several times in prison to tell him that Eli was unwilling to do anything to help in the various matters Carson faced as a convicted murderer. Essentially, she was a human firewall, which only caused Carson to treat her terribly whenever they were face to face.

Returning Carson to prison was a small pleasure for her, though she didn't let that on. Anything could wind up becoming a trigger for his anger and rage, and though she was paid well to manage and deal with his cantankerousness, she didn't want to do anything to set it off. She remained with the pilots for most of the flight, checking on Carson periodically as he sat bound to his chair in the passenger section of the shuttle. Having located the associate who aided in his escape to the Moon, she kept them separate, which made Carson instantly unpleasant. His displays of meanness reminded her of how different Eli was from his father. Though she tried not to engage him, there were certain matters she needed to address with him, delegated to her by Eli. Coming in to check on him, she sat down next to him and laid out what was to be their last encounter, starting off with pleasantries in a vain attempt to placate him.

"We are about twelve hours from Chicago. Is there anything I can have brought to you?"

Carson had been sitting bound for hours with nothing to do, and no freedom to move about the ship. "Yes, puppet. When you return to the Moon, and my son has had his fill of pulling your strings, tell him he's welcome. He's welcome for all the success he achieved from my discovery."

Nora feigned a smile. "I'm sure you've told him that already."

Nora knew that Carson was looking for an outlet and wanted to deliver Eli's message quickly so that she could be done with him forever. "Despite your warm regard for Eli", she said, "he asked me to deliver a message to you."

"How entertaining. The words of my son as told by his ventriloquist dummy. Well, what is it? What does my dog of a son have to say, dummy? Speak. Speak, you mindless sycophant."

Nora shot Carson a cold glare. "This is the last time you will be hearing from your son or myself. Once you are delivered back to the state penitentiary, you'll be on your own."

She watched as Carson stewed. He was never a man to hold anything back. After a hardy laugh, he dug back into her. "I have been on my own my entire life, puppet. I made my own way and spoon-fed everyone else along the way. *My* discovery built that fabulous city on the Moon you live in, and your boss, *my son*, is the man he is because *I* created his opportunities for him. No one helped me build my wealth, but they all helped me spend it on hefty education bills, and capital investments. *You* are just a toy programmed to speak on command. Frankly, I don't give a damn if I don't see you again. I'll gladly die without having the annoyance of your company. As for my son, let me program a message for you to deliver to him. Tell him he can go to hell. And that when he gets there I'll greet him with a kick in his ass. I'm sure he'll have something to say then, when he needs his old man to keep him out of the flames." Carson leaned closer to Nora, eyes fixed on hers and as sharp as his tongue, and delivered his final words for his son with an unwavering voice. "The devil is going to be impressed when I'm finished showing him how it ought to be done."

His stare, locked on Nora, backed up his words. She could sense the evil in him looking for all the ways out it could find. But she wasn't going to sit any longer and be an outlet. "Goodbye, Mister Quest. Enjoy what is left of your life on Earth. I hope you took the time to see it for what it is, and not what you made of it."

She stood up and walked away, heading back to the shuttle's cockpit to ride the remainder of the trip as far away from Carson as she could. She wished she could sit him on the wing or send him the rest of the way adrift like a piece of space garbage.

As she sat back down in her chair behind the shuttle commander, she shook her head and rolled her eyes. Carson Quest didn't matter to her. Eli, however, meant a lot. When they first met, his outlook on life and humanity was, to her, unique. His early career focused heavily on creating prosperity for mankind; the robotics division at QuestCorp was developed to improve the daily lives of working men and women, and the medical research coming out of his company had eradicated two major diseases. He was smart enough to make money along the way, but his ultimate goal was to propel mankind forward into a more equalized existence. One of shared prosperity. These were things Nora couldn't help but love about Eli.

But his perspective had shifted after Chris Wu's accident. It bothered her. A little time on Earth would give her some measure.

8

Eli stood in front of Solomon Lal, an Ambassador visiting Moon City on an invitation sent to the Prime Minister of India. It was one of dozens of pitch meetings he had held in the weeks since unveiling the Demeter Initiative.

"No civilization has any chance of reaching full potential if it is based on a system of limited success. If the game is to get as much stuff as possible before all the stuff is gone, then the game is just a distraction from the fact that, in the end, everyone will lose. Wealth and poverty are two ends of the same spectrum, dual outputs of the same system, and for the bulk of Earth's societies, the one fundamental truth pushing them along and carving them into one category or the other is access to resources. Humanity has no chance of becoming its greatest rendition without having the ability to break free from this bondage. Since our current course is exploitation and exhaustion of natural resources with no new course viably set forth, our lack of options will inevitably cease the advancement of the human species. This is the driving force behind the Demeter Initiative."

Solomon Lal, renowned as a boastful and proud man, politely listened to Eli while waiting for his turn to speak. "Mister Quest, I sympathize with your position. I understand that all the circumstances that different groups of people endure in their lives dramatically alter outcomes, but it has always been this way. I don't know that simply adding in another source for energy would do very much to alter the natural course of mankind."

Lal's presence annoyed Eli. His visit was a consolation prize compared to the main event Eli was hoping for in meeting with the Indian Prime Minister. Eli was making strides in selling his energy program to world leaders, but it worked best when the leaders themselves were present to make the decisions. Lal was just hot air and posturing.

"Ambassador, we live in an era when currency simultaneously fills and sustains needs. People don't look to the stars when their heads are down, and they're working like dogs just to eat and stay out of the cold. Mankind will never unify if it is too busy chasing after basic needs. QuestCorp's Demeter Initiative can deliver all your country's food and power needs, indefinitely. How advanced would your country be if more people could spend time learning and building instead of farming or mining?"

"I want nothing more than stability and opportunity for every citizen in my country, Mister Quest, but to thrive beyond the Earth's supply is not a future anyone has ever faced before. In my experience, unknowns usually bring chaos and confusion, not enlightenment and advancement. What you are attempting is revolutionary, but revolution hasn't always worked out favorably. I think, in your great vision, you are looking too hard at possibilities, and not enough at practicalities."

Eli could see that a trip to meet the Prime Minister herself would be necessary, but since Lal was already in his office he pressed on with his argument, knowing it would reach the Prime Minister through Lal before Eli could deliver it. "I disagree with your assessment, Ambassador. Before I built Moon City, I spent many evenings working at my desk, gazing out above the New York skyline at the few stars bright enough to outshine the vibrancy of the sprawling city. I saw the metaphor. The world's greatest city, shining so bright that it almost blotted out the stars. Almost. The truth is, those stars that shone through the lights of the city will outlast it by millions or billions of years. Our greatest triumphs on this planet amount to nothing more than life in the dirt, and the chains of oil and soil that hold everyone to it. I can now give the world the power of the Sun. I believe that with that power we can build a civilization so much better than what we have already accomplished, and from it we will find a way to get to those shining stars and conquer them."

Ambassador Lal let out a loud, brief laugh. "I respect your beliefs, Mister Quest, but you are a dreamer with wanderlust if you think mankind will conquer the stars one day."

Eli grew stern. "Ambassador, please give the Prime Minister my best, and let her know I'll be visiting her personally on my next trip to Earth. Good day."

"Yes, of course. You might want to pay a visit to General Singh before you do, however. He has made it clear to her that he will not permit anyone, including the Prime Minister herself, to allow your robot army into India. What is it that you call it? 'Swarm,' I believe? He is not convinced that it is only wired for relief work, and therefore its presence on our nation's soil will be considered a direct threat to our safety and our peace. Other nations may have bought your snake oil, but India is not like other nations."

The ambassador got up to leave but turned to say one last thing. "Please, give your father my best. He has done so much to help advance our country's agriculture." He shook Eli's hand and then left his office. Eli glared at him as he left.

Nora entered. "You look happy as always," she said with a smug, slanted smile.

"I don't know why I waste my time with bureaucrats. I shouldn't have accepted the Prime Minister's offer to meet with *him* in her place. From now on, don't send me anyone but decision makers."

"It looks like he just made a decision."

Eli glanced at Nora from the corner of his eye, his face as stern as usual. "I'll get India. I'm not worried. How was your visit home? Fergus did terribly as your replacement while you were gone, as always."

"There are more important things to discuss right now. News is buzzing. Your entry into the energy market is shaking things up. The global economy isn't looking all that firm right now. The pushback on the Demeter Initiative is going to come sooner than you thought, and media coverage on S.W.A.R.M. isn't good; particularly from Emilia Trust. If I was guessing, I'd say she is trying to make up for lost time, since you had her S.W.A.R.M. exclusive based on Edward's leak pulled by the newspaper's board before it was published."

"It doesn't matter. The world has seen what we can do. When things get bad, everyone will want us on their side. They won't survive otherwise. The world needs to realize that S.W.A.R.M. is a force for good. Send out a press release reemphasizing *Semiautomated Worker Automaton Relief Management*. Make some food drops in areas impacted by famine. Find a disaster for S.W.A.R.M. to aid. I don't care if you have to create one. I want everyone to know the good will of the Sun as it is handed out to the world by our benevolent robots. They need to think of us when the time comes."

Nora's face filled with apprehension. "What is that supposed to mean?"

"Don't be concerned." He smiled at Nora, as if to signal he was being jovial, or joking around. Then, stern-faced once again, added, "Don't leave Moon City."

"Why?"

"That is all, Nora. Welcome back."

9

Emilia Trust was talking to her colleague, Brant, in the *News Today* office. The whole staff had been called in for a big meeting. The break from her work annoyed her, but the chance to bounce her thoughts off her peers wasn't wasted. "The freedom and independence realized through the Demeter Initiative was brought onto the world too quickly and in an unbalanced way. Even though we are months into QuestCorp's deployment of S.W.A.R.M. to implement new infrastructure for the Demeter Initiative, the whole thing is still widely unaccepted. And it's failing. Chaos is sweeping the globe, and *News Today* needs a better plan to cover it," she said, waiting for the meeting to begin.

"Sure," said Brant. "Try telling that to Tommy though. He's had a strong hold on our content lately. More than ever before. Don't say anything to piss him off today, okay? I don't want him to get going. You know how he gets."

Emilia continued as if she didn't even hear her co-worker. "Industries as well as countries are destabilizing because of the Demeter Initiative. Speculations are wreaking havoc on economies worldwide. Tommy needs to let us open up on this. Did you know he had me covering U.N. meetings last week? Give me a break."

Emilia was tuned in to how QuestCorp's "good intentions" were invariably turning the world on end. Tommy Whitcomb, the editor-in-chief for *News Today*, had called the meeting for the whole staff. To Emilia, there was no other story than the Demeter Initiative. She wanted to let Tommy know she wasn't going to sit under his thumb any longer. As he entered the room, she took a deep breath, and braced for what could easily be an ugly confrontation between them.

"Thanks for coming in everyone. I appreciate the fact that you are all busy and have deadlines and sources to meet, but today we must face the future of our business. I'm sure many of you have seen the writing on the wall that one-by-one newspapers are going down. Print is dead, and *News Today* isn't an exception. We must change in every way we can, and we need to do it yesterday. We need to become a mass media outlet. We need to be a destination for information that is available 24/7, with total access, and we must be faster than lightning when it comes to breaking news to the world. There is a lot going on out there and people want to hear about it. We need to give them the facts as well as tell them what to do with them. That's how it's all packaged now, for better or for worse. We need to be content-based and ground breaking at the same time, and we need to do it online, in social media, and in print for the few souls left on the bus without a smartphone. This is coming from the Board, and they've asked me to get you all in line with the changes immediately. I can't say I am thrilled with how news is presented these days, but for the survival of our business I agree that these changes need to happen. And, at the end of the day, I know each and every one of you will uphold your integrity. Now, I told the Board we are the best and that we can do anything. We just have to figure out a new way of doing what we do and multiply that by a hundred. So, who's got ideas?"

The room full of people who ask questions and find answers for a living was eerily silent. Looking around the room at her colleagues, Emilia rolled her eyes at their aversions to innovation, and called out to Tommy. "Is this really why you called us all in, Tommy? The world is going to shit, and we have to worry about the Board? We already have departments for everything you are talking about. Social media, digital exclusives—"

"—yes, Emi, we are already connecting with people digitally. All the channels are open, and all the tools are in place. What we need to do as reporters is become the brand; each and every one of us needs to become a specialist, an authority, an expert in the field, and a household name. We need to jam our stories into their eyes through multiple media platforms. We need to make people feel like it'd be worse than cheating on their spouses to even think about going anywhere else for the news. And, *everything* is news now. We have to become the only conversation worth having."

Emilia was awestruck by Tommy's message. He was usually the man who beat doors down to expose the story no one could see. She didn't understand why he was hung up about revamping the news department when the world was sliding onto thin ice. Looking around the room, she could see that the team did not meet Tommy's enthusiasm. "I'm sorry, sir," she said. "But shouldn't we be focusing on how the paper is going to cover QuestCorp's power revolution?"

Tommy pursed his lips. "Well, *that's* your job, as well. I expect that is what you all will be doing. Power from hydrogen fuel cells is a big story. People are curious, confused, and hungry for answers. However, think of all the people who will be coming online now that power and food aren't their daily grind. These people need to be *our* audience instead of someone else's. Our company's new direction is to become an embassy of knowledge to the many minds out there looking to learn, so you've got to become gurus on everything from nuclear physics to making pancakes. It's a new world, people. Time to get used to it."

Tommy then ended the meeting. Emilia, a skeptic with a penchant for conspiracy theories, was already ringing the silent alarms about where the world was headed. Eli Quest had never been, in her mind, a hero of any kind; heroes didn't save the world with business deals and contracts. To her, he was a businessman, nothing more. All the good work his company was doing out in space was falling apart on the ground, yet his robot army was still implementing the Demeter Initiative as though there weren't any problems. It didn't add up that the world might reach the edge of bliss at the hands of a hard-nosed business tycoon. Regardless of *News Today's* new direction, Emilia had her own story that she wanted to break.

10

Edward and Elena were walking through the farm in Moon City. It emulated farms back on Earth, with large open pastures, and stables for livestock. Cows and chickens roamed freely in the pasture that edged the dirt path they walked along as a simulated Earth sky shone down on them from a dome above lined with video tiles. The smell of manure aside, it was a charming place Edward and Elena would often visit to forget the crammed confines of the ICS or their sterile desks. Since Eli shut down the ICS though, the two had been overseeing more of the Demeter Initiative's operations.

Along their walk, Edward confided in Elena, who was, among many things, his pillar of strength. "I don't want to do this anymore," he said to her in a tone of frustration. "I don't really like managing people, and I don't like having to give Nora progress reports to pass on to Eli. I am so much more useful than that. I think Eli is punishing me."

"For what?" Elena asked. "For Wu? *He* sent Wu in. Not you. He has no right to be mad at you."

"I know. I don't think he sees things that way though. I don't think he wants to blame himself, so he's made up his mind that the wormhole cache is the problem, and therefore I am responsible. It's ridiculous."

"It is. I agree. What do you want to do?"

Edward sighed and rubbed his face. "I don't know. I can't walk away from Eli; or QuestCorp at least. I've invested too much work here. I have to convince him to let us go back to work on the wormholes. The Demeter Initiative is just too messy right now."

"It is. Eli should have done more to prepare people for the program. The science is basic, the impact is positive. People just don't see it."

"Yes, well, it is, and it isn't. S.W.A.R.M. is revolutionary, but honestly, I don't understand why people fear it so much. If they could just look beyond and see the good it is doing in rolling out power and food to areas that had no chance on their own. People are people, I suppose."

Elena nodded as they walked along the pasture. "Your science is revolutionary, Edward. Eli's is borrowed. He'd be only half the success he is without you. Without the wormholes he wouldn't be able to bankroll S.W.A.R.M., the Initiative, or even Moon City probably. He'd be as limited as anyone back on Earth, and he knows that. So, he should know better than to mistreat you."

Edward nodded. "Yeah, sure, but I truly think he doesn't see it that way." He stopped walking and leaned against the fence that ran along the pasture. Elena followed. "I really think his focus on Wu getting injured in the cache has clouded his vision."

Elena got defensive. "Wu made the choice. He could have objected; we had the probe ready to go. Don't let Eli push Wu's accident on you. Don't accept fault for something you didn't do."

Edward sighed, and looked down at the grass. "I know. It's just an unfortunate thing. I mean, there was no way to know what the fourth dimension would do to him. Maybe we should have stopped him. We'd have saved him if we did. It's been months. He's not going to come out of it."

Elena placed her hand on Edward's arm and turned to him, looking him sincerely in the eyes. "Edward. You are a genius. You need to think about your science. Wu, the Demeter Initiative, it's distracting, and honestly, a waste of your time. If Eli doesn't see that, maybe it's time to move on. The world has seen what your mind can do now. Any of his competitors would be fortunate to have access to you."

Edward smiled as he gazed back into her eyes. "Thank you. I love you." He leaned over and gave her a small kiss.

"I know. I love you too. Come on." She motioned with a tilt of her head for them to resume their visit of the farm. They walked down the path past the cows and chickens, holding hands as they strolled.

11

S.W.A.R.M. faced a blockade from a battalion of General Singh's tanks near the India – Pakistan border, while Eli held and emergency meeting with the Prime Minister in the nation's capital.

"Madam Prime Minister, S.W.A.R.M. is a unified robotic super force, capable of operating humanitarian relief missions from start to finish without guidance, after receiving a solitary command order from a single control point, which is me. It is a force for good. Whether on a food distribution mission or a post-natural disaster search and recovery mission, once deployed, S.W.A.R.M. performs at a level never before seen in the areas of robotics or artificial intelligence, and does so *peacefully*. It is fully capable of making real-time decisions based on its own observations and assessments of any scenario while a precise level of coding ensures public safety."

"Mister Quest, there is no emergency here in my country, and if there were, we would be completely capable of managing it. Your robot army has no need or authority to be here."

Eli wasn't looking to mince words. "Madam, for months S.W.A.R.M. has been used all over the world to roll out the Demeter Initiative. Now our resources have been requested by your fellow statesmen and we are merely trying to deliver our product. *Peacefully*."

The Prime Minister grew impatient. "I will not allow it. My fellow statesmen can dream all they want of robots and power. I say what comes and goes for my country, and we do not want your brand of chaos here, peaceful or not."

Eli returned hostilities. "Madam, I have met resistance to this program in wealthy nations, where the profiteers of prosperity and success routinely fight to maintain the status quo. And I knew before launching the Demeter Initiative that undermining economic stability and financial power with grossly inexpensive energy alternatives would not go uncontested in those parts of the world. But, let their loss be your gain. You have the opportunity to compliment your own growth with my technology, and amplify your results. In no time you can be operating on the same platform as the world's superpowers."

Eli paused. The Prime Minister sat silently with a look of frustration.

"Madam Prime Minister, your resistance to the future is capricious. During your campaign for office you promised your people that you'd bring them into the heart of the next century by leading with technology and innovation. There is no greater innovation in technology than the Demeter Initiative."

"Mister Quest, I will be blunt. I don't trust your claims of wanting to bring the world to new heights with this power you've obtained from the Sun. The Sun is everyone's. You have no right to sell it to them. I recognize that with the world's largest population, India has high demands for energy, and we will undoubtedly rely on your company to help meet those needs in some way. However, even though we will indeed need the help of a lot of people like you and from a lot of companies like yours, I will not be the one who agrees on behalf of the people of India to pay for the Sun."

"The Sun *is* everyone's. I agree. I am only bringing it down to them, so they can use it. Your people will be better off with it in their hands instead of hanging over their heads. All people will. Don't get left behind."

"I am not worried about being left behind. Everything comes and goes, and history collects it all. I want history to tell a story about how *India* changed the world, not your corporation. I want the next great discovery to come from *here*. My country. From Earth."

Eli saw the similarity between Solomon Lal and the Prime Minister, so he didn't expect to get anywhere with her either. "Supply on Earth will run out. If you're playing the game of getting as much stuff from it as you can before all the stuff is gone, then everyone you're playing for will lose in the end. The future will come from beyond what you can dig up or grow. It's time to move on."

"Life begins and ends with the earth. You can't move on from that fact."

Eli's quick-firing impatience loaded and deployed on the Prime Minister. "No, Madam, I can, and I have. And, I'll bet there are a lot more people like me in your country than there are like you."

"I am Prime Minister because the people chose me. I am the reflection of my country. Don't be surprised if you don't see yourself among them."

"I won't have the chance. I'm heading right back to Moon City. But, I'm keeping S.W.A.R.M. here to offer your people what you won't. We will see who is who in the end."

"I will not allow this."

"You have no choice."

"If your robot horde tries to mobilize, I will have it destroyed."

Eli stood from his seat facing the Prime Minister's desk, and with a look of solid conviction, gave his final thoughts on the matter. "We will see," he said before walking out of her office.

12

Nolan Keller watched his mother, Mariel, as she tended herbs in the side yard along the homestead on Keller Farm. She hadn't noticed him while gardening, but he was content to be silent and watch her work. It was a familiar sight, and one that went way back into his childhood. When she stood up to stretch, she finally spotted him standing next to the old tire swing along the edge of the yard bordering the cornfields. He was pushing the swing gently with his finger, smiling at her.

"I remember when your father first put that swing up for you," she shouted. "You were so happy. You said you couldn't wait to fly in it."

Nolan smiled. Mariel walked over with open arms and embraced him with the kind of hug only a mother gives. "Hi, son. Welcome home."

"Hi, Mom. I missed you." Nolan pressed a gentle kiss on the top of her head.

"I missed you too. Felt like forever this time, Savior."

Nolan nodded. "Two months."

"That's the longest one yet. Must be a lot of people out there who need a hero." She looked intently at Nolan. There was a brief pause in which she looked deeply into his eyes, as if she was looking for the boy that disappeared so long ago. Nolan grew up fast after his father's death, a fact of which Mariel often expressed heavy guilt and regret. "How long are you going to stay?"

"I'm sorry, Mom. Not long. Things are rough out there right now." He watched as his mother's gaze dropped with disappointment.

"It's alright, I understand. I'm glad you came back for today." It was the anniversary of the death of her husband, Frank.

"I would never miss this day with you. How are you holding up?"

"I miss him. It's no different than any other day, but I'm glad we've faced this day together all these years. Your father was so amazing. He'd be so proud of who you've become."

Feeling uneasy, Nolan changed the subject. "Did you hear the latest about Carson Quest?"

Mariel let out a small laugh. "Yes. Escaped from prison in a wheelchair and then returned to prison by his own son. It just goes to show you that no one on Earth wants anything to do with that man. Nor does anyone on the Moon for that matter. But, today isn't about him. Today is about your father. Twenty years ago, today, I lost the great love of my life." Mariel looked at Nolan with tear swells in her eyes. "I'm sorry, Nolan. Sorry we never told you about the ship or your birth mother before that day. I feel guilty about that every day. So much loss for a child to bear."

Nolan had heard the same apology every year from his mother. "It's fine, Mom. What else could you have done? I appreciate why you kept me hidden from the world."

"We always thought we were doing the right thing. We knew you were different, and special, but we didn't know how the world would react. If I knew they were going to embrace you and call you "Savior" once they learned about the good in you, I would have sung your secret from the mountains!"

"I know. But, I like being Nolan. It's nice to have a way to turn it all off."

"Well, your secret will always be safe with me."

"Thanks, Mom. Do you want to visit Dad now?" Nolan asked, hoping to steer his mother away from a conversation that would only end in her tears.

"You should eat first. You just got here. Probably haven't eaten yet. Come inside. I'll heat something up."

Mariel and Nolan walked together into the old farmhouse. It had been standing on Keller Farm for over a century, dutifully cared for by generation after generation of Keller heart and soul. Nolan was the last Keller to be born on the farm, and the only child to his parents, Mariel and Frank.

When they reached the kitchen, Nolan sat down at the table. He watched as his mother grabbed some leftovers from the fridge, fired up the stove, and began effortlessly reheating a home-cooked meal. It was something he had watched her do thousands of times over the years, although this time he could see all those years weighing on her. His mother looked tired and old. She had been running the family farm and managing the staff since her husband was killed, and Nolan had heavy guilt that he wasn't around enough to do more for her. He was capable of so much, yet he often felt that it was never enough when it came to his parents.

"The farm looks great, Mom. The crops are really loving the weather this summer. I passed the south field on the way in. I saw you fixed the fence without me. I'd have done it for you if you—"

"—I know, I know, but you're busy, and the Tice twins needed some extra work. It didn't cost much to have them do it, and I like to help people when I can too, you know. Besides, harvests have been good. There are bigger problems in the world for you to worry about than our busted old fence posts. Did you hear about the robots in India this morning?"

"No. I've been in and out of some bad areas. I can't say I've heard it all. What happened? Is it bad?

Mariel let out a small laugh. "Is there something that Savior doesn't know? Good thing he has a Mama, then, to fill him in." Mariel smiled jokingly, and Nolan laughed.

"I feel like I've been everywhere trying to catch pieces," he said. "I've been able to help a lot of people though."

"Yes! I've read the articles. *News Today* covered all your missions and put them online. Wonderful stories. You bring hope to so many people, Nolan."

"I wish I could do more."

"You save lives. Every day. That's enough, even for someone like you. This shake-up started by Eli Quest isn't helping anything. This morning the news said that he sent his robots to India, yet they were stopped by the Indian army."

Nolan took a bite of some homemade bread his mother had put out on the table. "I didn't hear that. How'd it play out?"

"It was something, let me tell you. The Indian army blockaded QuestCorp's army of robots in a mountain pass. They were carrying so many crates of food and water, and all those power cells they've been installing all over too. It was on all the networks. Live. Everywhere. The whole world must have seen it. Word must have reached that army because eventually they just let the robots pass. It was unsettling to see."

"It's a little crazy everywhere right now, Mom."

"I know. It's this Demeter program; all this new power and food. Used to be that you needed to plant things in the dirt to make food. That you needed to farm. What is Eli Quest gonna do once he has fed the hungry? Go out of business? You know that won't happen. No, he'll turn his efforts toward making food for everyone, and put honest working farmers like us out on our butts. He's almost as bad as his father." She walked to the table, put down two plates of meatloaf, potatoes, and collards, and then sat to eat with Nolan.

"The farm's not going anywhere today, Mom. Or tomorrow. I've never thought of Eli Quest as the model citizen type, but I don't think he is trying to put farmers out of work. Despite the turmoil his company has caused, the principles behind it seem genuine. I understand wanting to help people. He just took the wrong approach. He's someone who has always had things his way, never had to struggle. That's why he doesn't really know how to fix the problems people face. His hydrogen technology is better than the alternatives right now as far as I can tell, though. It's cleaner than fossil fuels, and faster and more capable than renewable energy. QuestCorp is right about this; the world just doesn't seem to be ready for it."

"That's a pretty gracious assessment coming from the man who is cleaning up the mess."

"If it wasn't Eli Quest's mess, it would be someone else's." Nolan picked up his fork and knife and began cutting into his food. "Let's eat. We should really get to the cemetery before it gets dark."

The two ate their dinner together and then left for the cemetery. Visiting his father's grave every year was hard for Nolan. He was nearly a teenager when his dad was murdered but was already in control of most of his abilities. He felt like he should have been there to save his father, and he had been trying to make up for it ever since. Nolan had become the hero he felt he should have been for his father that night, but it didn't lessen his feelings of guilt and loss.

As they paid their respects at the gravesite, Mariel held Nolan's arm tightly. They stood in silence and both remembered Frank in their own way. Nolan's mother was always the one who was there to take care of him and help him with the struggles he faced growing up different, but to Nolan, his father was a hero. He showed his heart, always knew what to do, and could fix anything. He never walked away from anything without giving it his full effort first, and in doing so rarely walked away from anything at all. After the silent memorial, Nolan and Mariel drove most of the way back to the farmhouse in silence, until she ended the quiet with a question.

"What do you think about QuestCorp stealing from the Sun, Nolan?"

"What do you mean by stealing, Mom?"

"I mean the harvesting. If the Sun gives you your powers—"

"—we don't know that, Mom. It could be the air for all we know."

Mariel rolled her eyes. "Okay, but still, are you worried that the Sun's being taken and made into things? What if they use too much? At least with farming you can replenish the soil. What if he takes so much it effects how all the plants grow? They need the Sun to make their food."

Nolan considered his mother's question briefly. "I haven't really thought about it, to be honest. According to QuestCorp, harvesting started years ago. Things don't seem any different if that's what you mean. I don't think anything they are doing will affect things here on Earth, biologically I mean."

"I think you should give it some thought. I don't want something crazy to happen, and then I lose you too."

"Mom. I'm not going anywhere."

"I know, I know," Mariel said before abandoning the conversation, smiling at Nolan before turning to look out the window at the passing landscape.

The rest of the ride home continued in silence. Once home, Mariel said goodnight, and went to her bedroom. Nolan was leaving early the next morning, so he went to bed as well. He walked upstairs to his old room to get some sleep. He took off his gear and draped it over the closet door. He settled into his old bed and stared up at the ceiling, hoping to let his thoughts drift away so he could fall asleep. Nolan enjoyed the solitude that came with the night because it helped him close himself off from the world for a while, much like a flower that closes in the night. On this night, however, thoughts about all the people he had recently saved and fights he had won mixed with thoughts about his mother and father. He closed his eyes and remembered the story his mother told him the night his father was killed.

'Nolan, your Dad was in that field tonight protecting a secret. It's something we always wanted to tell you but couldn't find the right way or the right time. It's a secret that explains why you are so different from everyone else. One day I was planting mums along the base of the front porch when a shooting star fell out of the sky, shaking the ground and filling the sky with smoke and fire. Your father came running out of the house and before I could recount to him what I saw we were racing away in his pickup truck, headed for the cornfields and chasing down that star. When we caught up to it we couldn't believe what we saw. There was no star. No meteor had fallen, and it wasn't a plane crash or anything like that. We had chased down a spaceship, which lay in pieces all over the field. When it crashed it left a scar in the dirt, hundreds of feet long, scattering debris everywhere. The hull of the ship was broken wide open, almost entirely in half, and within the wreckage wires and pipes popped and sizzled. Inside the ship was a woman, one like I had never seen before. Her feathery, black hairpiece lay on the ground next to her and her head and skin, all paper-white, looked alien, as did her pitch-black eyes. Not just the pupils, or the irises, but every inch of her eyes were as black as a starless night. They were open, tearful, and staring out of the wreckage at me. Frozen in fear, I felt like I couldn't even breathe. I stared back at her for what felt like days before I noticed her movements; tiny breaths followed by convulsions from intense pain. Then I noticed her belly and realized that the convulsions were actually contractions.

I sent your father to the truck for water and blankets while I maneuvered into the wreckage to get to her. When I got to her I saw just how beaten and bloody she was from the crash, how weak her breathing sounded, and that her words, so faintly spoken, were indiscernible, not for their faintness, but for their being of a language wholly unfamiliar. I held her hand and touched her face and told her it would be alright. She seemed to understand. Your father came back from the truck as resolute as always, and together we helped the woman from outer space deliver her baby.

I was amazed by the birth. It wasn't all that different than what a human would go through. The baby, a boy, came along quickly, and looked like his mother; dark eyes and paper-white skin. Yet, he began changing the moment he was born. With his first breath of Earth's air the color of his skin changed. He cried as any newborn would, but there was no umbilical cord to cut. After wrapping him in a blanket we handed him to his mother, and despite how weak she was, she smiled at the sight of her son. She then said a word from her own language, "No…Lan," naming him before losing her strength and fading away. I took the baby from her and held him close, looking down on him in my arms. "Nolan," I repeated, soothing him as he cried. He stopped crying and opened his eyes, all black, just like his mother's. The Sun shining overhead reflected in each of the child's eyes, and as he looked up at it, his eyes began to change, turning a blazing shade of red. As quickly as the red blaze came it faded, clearing away to reveal a pair of blue eyes, just like a newborn human baby's, sharp and beautiful. Your Dad and I loved you from that moment, Nolan."

Nolan opened his eyes and noticed his mother standing in the doorway to his room. A slight smile poorly masked her look of sorrow. She glanced at the closet door where he had hung his gear, mostly intact but for some tears and punctures in between the armor plates.

"I remember making your first suit like it was yesterday," she said. "Spandex. You wanted blue, but black and white were the only colors they had in the material. I'm glad I chose black. Who knows how dirty the white would have gotten with all the things you used to get into. As silly as it may have looked at the time, it was the only fabric that wouldn't tear up when you started electrifying and teleporting."

Nolan smiled at the memory. "I remember. Dad was so mad when you cut out the upholstery from the back of the bench seat in his truck to make the boots."

Mariel laughed. "Yes, he was, but it was strong stuff. Years driving around the farm on that upholstery and it never cracked or tore. It was the only material I could sew to the rubber soles we made from old tires and not bust a stitch. They held up well for a long time."

"I had to repair them now and then, but they held together."

"It was a great suit for you. I didn't like it when you switched to all that tactical armor stuff. Yet, it's how the world knows you now so who am I to say anything?"

Nolan smiled, and laughed. "It's durable. It handles teleportation jumps and battles. Don't you remember my old suit and clothes smoldering after a jump?"

"Don't remind me. As strong as you are I never liked that."

"Well, now you don't have to worry. The gear holds up. It's fire resistant and the rubber in the gear helps with all the electricity," Nolan said, as if he'd just won an argument.

"I'll always worry, Nolan. I'm your mother. It doesn't matter what you do, you still have a heart that can break the same as anyone else. I worry most about that."

"Mom, I'll be fine."

Mariel looked away, fighting back tears. "I'd ask what time you are leaving in the morning, but I know you'll be gone before I can see you off. Goodnight, son. Thank you for being here today."

"Good night, Mom." Nolan closed his eyes to fall asleep as his mother turned to head back to her room. He let out a sigh as he thought about what he would face in the morning, and then rolled over to fall asleep.

13

Above the horizon, framed by the infiniteness of space, Earth hung glowingly in quietude. Outside Eli's office window, various robots and rovers whirred about, quietly performing their mundane tasks. Eli enjoyed watching them. They were almost invisible pieces of his cosmic empire, yet still contributed to his success.

Eli looked out his office windows at the gravity-defying architecture of his city that relentlessly spanned the moon. Despite being built on a barren landscape of colorless rock and dust-littered craters, the views from Moon City illuminated the beauty of its pristine environment. The emptiness of the Moon captivated Eli, who thought of it as a sort of last wilderness. It was a place that didn't owe anyone anything and had nothing much to give. Yet, he staked his claim on it, and from it he was changing the world.

His vision to elevate mankind beyond Earth's limitations was a gargantuan task, one that took the resources of this solar system and beyond to accomplish. The unknowns surrounding the event that injured Chris Wu was a complication amid his plans, and it weighed heavily on him and his temperament. As he stood at the window waiting for Nora, he thought about how she'd become uneasy around him, a dynamic that was entirely new.

She spoke immediately upon entering his office. "How was India?"

"Fine. Eventually. What do you have for me?" He continued to look out the window as he spoke.

"A war has started," she said matter-of-factly. "India and Pakistan. India is holding them to blame for S.W.A.R.M. entering their country."

"It doesn't matter. If things seem bad, it's only because they can be better. This is just a rough start."

"Well, do you think maybe you could clue some people in down there? Do you have a plan to undo the chaos the Demeter Initiative has caused? We all could use one!" When she realized Eli wasn't going to answer, she continued. "How about at least filling me in? I thought this whole initiative was going to make things better. I've told you a dozen times now that it isn't."

Eli finally turned to face Nora. "Be patient. And don't forget who you are speaking to." Eli's face said more than his words, though. "Sit down, and I will enlighten you." Nora sat, and Eli continued. "My plan isn't about making the world better. It's about making mankind better. I am going to elevate the human race by moving it to a better world."

Nora was speechless. Eli pressed on, noting her reaction. "Acquiring that ship from Keller's Farm unlocked science and innovations that were a century away from reality. It also showed me how behind the human race is. As such, uplifting the world so that all can enjoy it equally is a fool's errand. Eventually, Earth will cease to provide. The Demeter Initiative overcomes this problem, but I am not willing to gamble that after I am gone it will continue to be humanity's safeguard. A new planet has been selected for resettlement that will provide for mankind indefinitely. Earth is holding us back."

Nora's eyes widened in disbelief. "Eli, you sound insane. None of this makes sense. You can't just move the human race! You have no way of—"

"—I do. I do have a way of moving them. I'm sorry that I haven't told you all of this before. I wanted you to have one last trip home on your own terms before I told you."

Eli's attempted thoughtfulness was overlooked as Nora grew furious. "What the hell is your plan, exactly? Are you going to just convince the entire world to get up and go? You can't even convince me to like it here on the Moon!"

"I am not giving them a choice," Eli said bluntly.

"What is that supposed to mean?"

"Nora, as much as there is good out there in the universe, there is just as much that is bad. Wormhole after wormhole has confirmed this; it will take very little to destroy what is here. I know this because I have found it." Eli paused briefly. "I am going to kill Earth. When people realize the only chance they have to stay alive is QuestCorp, leaving Earth will be an easy sell."

Tears began to well in Nora's eyes as she struggled to find words. "You…you can't—"

"—I can. I specialize in finding ways to do all the things that can't be done."

Nora fought back with the few words she could pull together. "You can't. The world won't let you. Savior won't let you."

"Savior will not be a roadblock on the path to a superior mankind," he said, smiling sadistically.

Nora's face filled with grief. "I can't believe this. I can't believe you."

"You have doubts?"

"No."

"Savior is an alien, an invasive species. I won't stand aside and watch him upset mankind's future as he did its present. The human race needs to sort itself out. It doesn't need help from a demigod only interested in saving the weak. We won't become stronger if they continue to survive. I don't want him interfering once we begin our transcendence."

"You try to make yourself sound noble, but you're just a killer. You're just like your father."

Eli became enraged. "I will bring a future that shines so bright that no one will be able to see *his* grave in the shadows behind us. I am nothing like my father. He killed a man on a hunch. I am setting mankind free."

Nora sat, crying. Eli had crushed her world, even though the worst of his plan was yet to come. She closed her eyes and took a deep breath. Gaining some composure, she stood slowly and cast him a look of unsteady defiance.

"Good bye, Elijah," she said, and then walked away.

14

Eli pushed open the door to the medical bay where Chris Wu was being treated. Wu had been in a coma since the accident, and Eli's best doctors had been unsuccessful in treating him. Randomly, Wu had fits where he would ramble on uneasily about his experience, but for the most part remained unconscious and unresponsive. Eli had Nora deliver him daily updates on Wu's condition, but it didn't look like that was going to happen anymore.

When Eli entered the room, one of the doctors treating Wu happened to be at his bedside adjusting his blood pressure monitor. "What's changed?" he asked, his brusqueness catching the doctor off guard. "What progress have you made, Doctor Philips?"

Philips was the main doctor overseeing Wu's care. "There is no change, Eli. He is no better today than he was yesterday, or the day he arrived." He started to write notes on Wu's chart, turning away from Eli as he did.

"Is he still talking in his sleep?"

"He is."

"Anything new? Revealing?"

Doctor Philips turned to face Eli. "He is still saying that he is inside out and that he's been blinded. However, since he is verbalizing his thoughts from a coma, please take them with a grain of salt. Whatever happened to him left his subconscious with some heavy demons to battle, but we can't mistake that for reality. As I've said before, this is a very atypical case, and unfortunately there is nothing we can do to awaken him."

"I want him awake. DO MORE!" Eli shouted.

Philips paused and swallowed, then wiped the sweat from his brow. "There is nothing more to do. Sometimes people wake up from comas. Sometimes they don't. We don't even know how to treat Doctor Wu because we don't know what actually happened to him. All we have to go on is his current condition, which is unique to begin with."

"Doctor, you haven't done all you can. It's time to get aggressive."

The doctor slammed Wu's chart down on the floor, which caught Eli by surprise. "Electroconvulsive therapy will not help. We are *not* going to do that!"

Eli looked at Philips sternly. "Do not forget who you are speaking to, Richard. I can end your career with a phone call so do as you are told. I have no patience left today. Pick up your clipboard and call in your staff."

"No. Absolutely not. What you are asking could damage whatever is left of his scrambled mind."

Eli glared at the doctor who was standing tall. "I want results."

The doctor shook his head and threw up his hands. "No," he repeated.

Eli pursed his lips as his brow tightened. "Very well. You are dismissed. I hope you enjoy farming or selling insurance."

Doctor Philips glared at Eli, shaking his head in disgust as he walked out of the medical bay. Eli then walked into the hall and yelled toward a nearby doctor. "You. What's your name?" The doctor stammered. "Never mind," Eli said. "Where is the ECT machine?"

The doctor quickly looked at a humble machine on a pushcart, and then looked back at Eli.

"Bring it in," Eli commanded, but the doctor didn't move. Eli sighed. "Fine," he said. "I'll get it myself. You can go join Doctor Philips on his farm."

Eli grabbed the ECT machine and began rolling into Wu's room.

"Mister Quest, you can't do this!" The doctor grabbed onto Eli's arm and tried to pull him to a stop. Eli swung a fist and struck the doctor square on the nose. He was unconscious before he even hit the ground. Eli wheeled the machine into the room and over to Wu's bedside where he began hooking up the electrodes to Wu's forehead. He then placed a leather strap in Wu's mouth, and turned on the ECT machine. He turned the dial to eight hundred milliamps and released an electrical charge. A powerful surge entered Wu's frontal lobe. His body seized until the surge stopped. Wu relaxed, and Eli leaned in to look for signs of life. Wu remained still. Eli hit him again, shocking him for six seconds the second time. He saw no change. Eli sat down in a chair near Wu's bedside. He sighed, rubbing his face with his hands while contemplating the situation. He glanced at the machine, then grabbed the control dial and turned it up to one thousand milliamps.

"Come on, Wu," he said. "Come back to me." He fired off another shock into Wu. Ten seconds. Nothing. Ten more. "COME ON!" He shouted, pushing the machine onto the floor. The electrodes attached to Wu ripped off and whipped to the floor as well. Eli sat back down, letting out a scream through his clenched teeth. He looked at Wu, somewhat slumped over to one side in the bed, then let out a heavy sigh.

A heavy sigh then came from Wu.

Eli sprung up. Wu's eyes were open and staring up at the ceiling. "Chris! I…I…welcome back."

Wu smiled at Eli. "Welcome back," he said, starting to laugh under his breath.

Wu's behavior quickly turned Eli's surprise to concern. "Talk to me," he said. "What did you see? What did this to you?" He asked, holding Wu's hand tightly. "Tell me!" He urged, leaning in so that he was face to face with Wu.

Wu didn't answer. He just continued to stare, his quiet laughter growing louder until it filled the medical bay.

15

The last day had come. Eli was sitting in his office in Moon City, alone, staring out at Earth. A series of monitor screens on his desk displayed surveillance video: one showed a live news report of Savior back on Earth, helping a bus full of people stuck in a flood somewhere, and another was a stationary view of Wu in his bed in the infirmary. The sound was muted, but Eli wasn't paying them any attention anyhow. As he viewed the Earth he rubbed his thumb back and forth along the edge of a remote control. It had only a single button. One push of the button meant everything mankind had ever known was over, and that it would be forced to circle a new star on a planet that had been selected far off in another galaxy. There was no right time to push the button; no countdown, or computation to make. He just had to push it and become mankind's new savior, but only after becoming its greatest villain first. He spoke into his watch. "Have you located Miss Reinhard?"

S.W.A.R.M. replied in a tinny voice. *'Negative. Nora Reinhard has not been located."*

"Keep searching."

"Affirmative."

As he sat with the remote in hand, Edward Martinez walked into his office. Through the reflection in the windows Eli saw him enter, and swiftly placed the remote in his pocket as he turned to Edward, whose face was pale, a tell that he had seen the remote before Eli had hidden it.

"Eli. Don't do this."

"Get out," Eli said bluntly.

"Don't destroy the Earth. Lead the people to a better world, but don't kill this one."

"GET OUT!" Eli turned back toward the window, but Edward didn't leave.

"This isn't what we've worked so hard for."

"Yes, Edward, it is. You just never knew it. How lucky for you Nora clued you in before she left."

"And what about Nora then? Do you think you'll be able to find her once it has all started?"

Eli's body stiffened with tension. "She knows the plan. She chose to leave. If I find her, I find her."

"Don't do this. Please! Gather up the people. Transport them to the new planet. Start a superior mankind out there among the stars. But, leave the Earth for those who wish to stay."

Eli turned and looked squarely into Edward's eyes. "How many people do you think would go if given a choice? Don't be naïve."

"You can't force people into this."

"Enough. Is the wormhole ready? Has it been extracted from the cache?"

"The wormhole's not ready. Arthur won't unlock it. We can't identify what within it affected Wu, and although he's awake, he's not telling us anything useful. Extracting anything from the cache just isn't safe right now."

"You pleaded with me to be put back to work on the wormholes. You should be working on a safe way to access and use them right now, Edward. Not here pleading to me over other matters."

Edward's face grew even paler. "Eli, Elena and I want to be back on the ICS, but not for this. We don't—"

"—I have assigned it to you. Your theories created the mess in the fourth dimension, so you should be able to fix it. Figure it out."

"My theories didn't consider the dangers of the fourth dimension that we understand now. With some time, I'm sure I can sort it all out, if Wu gets better and Arthur gives me access, but this crazy plan of yours is just too much of a pressure to work under."

"GET IT DONE!"

"I'm sorry, Eli. I can't. Elena and I would like to return to Earth. Whatever you are going to do, we don't want a part in it anymore."

"You will go back to work getting me the wormhole I need, or I will ship you both to Mars permanently where you can spend your days reinventing mining drills for the mining drones there. You no longer have control of your own fate, Edward. Nor does Elena. You have been chosen for a superior cause. Don't make me regret that choice."

"No." Edward stood defiantly before Eli.

Eli scowled as he stared back at Edward. He grabbed the remote from his pocket and pushed the button. Through the window behind him, Edward watched in horror as dark clouds began forming at several locations on Earth, pouring across the sky, flooding the atmosphere with a black, opaque cover that sprawled out in every direction. Slowly the clouds found one another and merged, obscuring Earth under a cloak of impenetrable darkness.

"That is all, Edward," Eli said. "Now get to work. You don't have a lot of time."

Edward looked at Eli, shocked. Eli stared back, then glanced at the door, signaling Edward to leave. Unable to find composure, Edward backed out of Eli's office and stood in the hall, staring with his mouth agape at what was now an unrecognizable planet hovering beyond the Moon's horizon.

"That is all, Edward" Eli said again.

Tears streamed down Edward's face as he snapped out of his daze, hearing Eli's words. He looked at Eli one last time before turning to head down the hall, his every step seemingly weighted.

Eli turned to view the Earth for himself. His eyes widened and he himself stood astonished by the sight, but only momentarily. He turned away, and looking down at the floor, spoke aloud. "I'm sorry, Nora."

He placed the remote on the corner of his desk and sat in his chair, the Earth darkly resting in the view behind him.

16

Dark clouds were filing in over Savior's head, but he didn't notice them. He was chest deep in rising floodwater from a levy that had breached nearby. Several cars and a bus evacuating the area were on the interstate, caught in the fast-moving flow of water rushing over the landscape. Savior was standing next to a nearly submerged SUV with a family of four trapped inside. The water was rushing in quickly, and the father was frantically working to unbuckle his toddler from a car seat in the rear passenger seat. Panic and the force of the water seemed to impede him. Savior held a hand out to grab the children and rush them to safety, but the water was rising faster than the children could be handed from the car. Noting the worsening conditions, he reached into the vehicle, and pushed the father back into his seat. "Buckle your seatbelt," he said, and then dipped under the water. Immediately the SUV began to rise. Water spilled out of the opened windows as the vehicle was lifted out of the floodwaters. Soon, Savior's arms emerged from the water, holding the vehicle above him, followed by his head. Immediately, he began walking toward an embankment on the side of the highway that was above the floodplain, carrying the SUV and the family in it. He set the vehicle on higher ground, and then looked back to the bus that was still in danger.

Electricity surged around his body, and in a jolt he disappeared, reappearing instantly on top of the bus. He grabbed hold of the roof of the bus with his hands, the metal crumpling where he gripped it. One solid pull and a large portion of the roof peeled off. Water was already moving in at the passengers' feet. He jumped down into the bus and grabbed the woman closest to him.

"Hold on," he said to her. "This will hurt."

An electrical charge surged around them both, and in an instant, Savior teleported them both to the high embankment. The woman fell to the ground, a look of fright on her face. "It wears off quickly I'm told," he told her before jolting back to the bus to grab another person. Jolt after jolt, he rescued the passengers of the bus one at a time. With everyone safe, he watched as the flood overtook the vehicles left behind. He finally noticed the darkening sky. "You'll be alright here," he said to the crowd, and then charged up again, teleporting himself high into the sky.

Once in the air he was in a freefall, and saw the sky as it had never been before. He jolted higher up into the atmosphere, and was able to see dark, gassy plumes coming up from the ground in steady streams from multiple points on the Earth, feeding the dark clouds blotting out the Sun and sky. With a series of quick jolts, he moved through the sky toward one of the plumes in the distance, tracing it to its point of origin: a QuestCorp hydrogen distribution facility. He began a series of teleports downward toward the building for a closer look, but unexplainably lost his ability to charge his jumps as he neared the ground. With a fast and heavy landing, he crashed into the plaza within the building complex, crushing the pavement with a hard landing and sending out a dust cloud that obscured the view of the facility around him. The landing hurt, which was unusual, and in the cloud of dust he laid on the ground with a pain in his legs and back that he had never felt before. He felt nauseous and weak.

Something approached him that sounded like machinery. Through the darkness and dust, Savior saw dozens of illuminated eyes moving in toward him. S.W.A.R.M. robots. Dazed but aware, he got to his feet only to realize he was having trouble standing. Everything spun.

He heard a synthetic voice. *"Target acquired. Awaiting command."*

Another voice responded. "Swarm."

But this voice was different. Although this one came from the same radio or speaker within the robots, it was human.

Savior was already off balance and staggering when the first strikes from the robot force hit him, knocking him down hard. A barrage of metal kicks punted him mercilessly in a harsh and relentless beating. He tried to fight back but was thrashed by the robots' hurricane force and speed. He tried to charge and jolt up into the air, but it amounted to nothing more than a small leap upward. His ears rung and his vision blurred, as he realized his abilities were almost completely compromised. Using the last of his strength, Savior broke free and ran off to regroup, hurt and bleeding.

17

Immediately after the incident, Eli was on every television station and news outlet claiming the release of the gas was an act of sabotage; that experimental power cores being tested by QuestCorp in several of its facilities had been maliciously compromised. His message of controlling and repairing the damage was framed optimistically. He delivered the message assuredly, telling the world that S.W.A.R.M. would act as the face and facilitator of the company's world-saving efforts.

Nora watched Eli's address to the world on television, and scoffed when he said QuestCorp would be the world's savior in the challenging times ahead. She had been ready for the day Eli would kill the planet, which came swiftly, and not long afterward, Eli made his address and then disappeared. She knew he would not stop his plan to "brighten mankind's future," but it was still a shock to witness the dawn of perpetual night. It quickly pushed the people of Earth into a struggle of death and madness fit for Armageddon, and she could not escape the mayhem. She had chosen to accept that although she herself couldn't stop Eli from exacting his plan, she could help someone who could. Finding Savior and helping him stop Eli was *her* plan to save mankind. Finding him would be a challenge though, especially since Eli would be hunting both of them down. Staying alive in a world gone mad was an even more pressing task, though.

During the first days of darkness, alone and in fear of being hunted on a dying world, Nora became a ghost. She hid wherever she could, watched everything, moved often, and then repeated the steps time after time. If she needed something, she stole it from wherever she could as long as it wasn't already in someone else's hands. Having firsthand knowledge of QuestCorp's capabilities and S.W.A.R.M.'s ability to search and acquire gave her a half-step head start, but constant movement was her key to staying free. She covered herself in clothing that concealed her from head to toe. Luckily, S.W.A.R.M.'s heavy presence made it easy to spot. Nora knew that Eli would also have a network of spies working alongside S.W.A.R.M., so she trusted no one, though staying away from Eli and his network of eyes did fall second to hunger.

Scouting a looted bodega for any food she could find, she found a few cans of corn that had rolled under the bottom of a refrigerator. She was on her hands and knees, pulling the cans out when she heard footsteps on the broken window glass from the storefront windows behind her. She froze.

"What have you got there?" A man asked. She heard another man laughing, as if nervously, under his breath.

Nora jumped to her feet to face the men. They seemed like normal people, but circumstances meant everyone was a threat. "I found some canned goods," she said. "There's enough to share."

"Share with who? Share with you? I have enough people to share with already. Step back."

The man had no weapons that she could see, but his face told her what she needed to know. He looked desperate and angry, not a mixture she wanted to deal with. "Sure thing." She threw the canned food on the floor and backed away, hands out in front of her so that the men could see her palms. "Take them. They're yours."

As she backed up, the laughing man ran over to the cans, swiping them up and returning to the side of the other in a near single movement. The three of them stood in a stalemate stare.

"You have the cans. Now leave."

The angry man didn't flinch. His eyes were fixed on Nora. "What else have you got?" He asked.

"Nothing," she said. "I'm looking for food just like you. You just took all I have."

His stare didn't falter. "WHAT ELSE HAVE YOU GOT?"

Nora bolted to the back of the store and made it to the back room before one of them grabbed the back of her coat. She slipped out of it, stumbling into the back door in the process. Her body pushed against the crash bar and she spilled out into the alley. She kept going. The two men pursued. At first, she gained some ground, but she couldn't outrun them. One of the men tackled her to the ground just before she made it to the avenue. She screamed. "NO! Get off me! I don't have anything."

The man ignored her and began searching through her clothes, tearing at them so that the head scarf she was wearing came loose.

"STOP! STOP!" she cried. The man grabbed her by the shoulders and slammed her against the ground.

"SHUT UP! SHUT UP!" He yelled, and continued searching through her clothes. She tried to push him off, but the other man grabbed her arms and pinned them down.

"I don't have anything," she cried once more, closing her tear-filled eyes as they searched her. At that moment, the man stopped, and the other man let go of her arms. Nora opened her eyes and saw the two men on their knees with their hands high in the air. They were surrounded by a S.W.A.R.M. battalion, all of which were pointing arm-mounted guns at them.

A tin voice spoke. *"Nora Reinhard acquired. Awaiting command."*

There was silence at first, but then Nora heard Eli's voice come over an intercom on one of the robots. *"Bring her to Moon City."*

It sent her into a panic. "No! Wait! Eli. Eli, don't do this. Let me be. Let me stay here." She looked at one of the S.W.A.R.M. bots. "Tell him! Tell him I don't want to go!"

Eli spoke again through the intercom. *"I will hear what you have to say after you are back here on the Moon. S.W.A.R.M., execute command."*

"Affirmative." Two robots picked up Nora and began taking her away. The man who pinned her down spoke up.

"Hey, robot. You got any of that hydrogen food?" S.W.A.R.M. did not answer. The angry man spoke again. "Hey! I'm talking to you!" He picked up a piece of loose asphalt from the ally and hurled it at one of the S.W.A.R.M. bots, hitting it in the back. Every bot in the battalion turned instantly and opened fire, killing the man where he knelt. Nora watched in horror as they carried her away. Death came swiftly in this new world of night.

"Put me down! Let me go!"

S.W.A.R.M. did not acknowledge her. She writhed and kicked and struggled to get free, but the robot's vice-like hold was too strong. As she wore herself out, she looked around and noticed some people had gathered and were watching as she was hauled away by S.W.A.R.M. Others were looking at the man who had just been killed. She called to them.

"Help me! Please!" But the people just watched. Nora's heart crumbled. In that moment, her view of Eli, and of people, was redefined. She had experienced what his plan really meant to mankind, and what the response would be. Her body slumped as S.W.A.R.M. carried her off.

18

Carson Quest sat on the bed in his prison cell. A spotlight cast enough light through his barred window that he could see the stark items within it, but little else. A small, wind up clock read that it was midday, but the world outside was completely dark. As he looked up at his window he sat motionless, dazed as if hypnotized by the eternal night. At that moment the spotlight was his world. Footsteps could be heard within the prison nearby, but he paid them no mind. A voice beyond the light's reach finally broke his trance.

"FOUND IT!" The voice shouted.

Carson jerked to awareness, turning toward the voice beyond his cell. He called back, stuttering to get his words out. "G-good job! Bring it here. Let's see what we've got."

Out of the dark recesses of the prison, a man entered Carson's cell pushing a wheelchair. "Here's your wheels," he said.

Smiling faintly, Carson showed his appreciation. "Thank you, Sylas. Where'd you find it?"

"This one? Infirmary. I couldn't find yours. I got a new one instead."

Carson reached over and patted Sylas' hand as it rested on the handle of the chair. "Very well. At least we can get out of here now."

Sylas nodded. "The doors are wide open. Some security gates are down. I'll have to carry you through one area, but we can get out no less." He paused, looking at the spotlight coming through the window. "Into the night."

"Well, let's not wait. Please, help me into my chair."

Sylas lifted Carson off the bed with little effort and placed him neatly into the wheelchair. Carson sort of grunted as he shifted into place.

"Thank you, Sylas. Let's go."

"You got it," Sylas said, and pushed Carson out the cell.

The two travelled along a row of cells toward the end of the dark cellblock. There were no lights on inside the prison, although the spotlight shining outside cast enough light through the cell windows that the two could find their way. Some of the light from the spotlight shone upon the bodies of the men who didn't survive the previous night's riot.

"That was some crazy shit," Sylas said as he steered Carson around one of the bodies.

Carson didn't answer, he just stared at the body as long as it was in his view. They reached the end of the block, and as they pushed through the door into a long corridor, Sylas spoke again, breaking the silence.

"So, you really think Eli is gonna come and get you out of here? You never had anything nice to say about him before."

"He'll come," Carson said in a soft, somber voice.

"Yeah, well I hope he does. Moon City was nice when we were up there. I could get used to that. You really think he'll bring me there too?"

"Yes," Carson answered, a look of remorse on his face that Sylas couldn't see.

The two continued along the corridor until they came to a security gate that had been folded in half but was still secured in its place by two of its hinges and the lock. Sylas took Carson out of his wheelchair and sat him gently on the floor. He folded up the wheelchair and placed it down on the floor on the other side of the mangled gate. It banged loudly against the gate sending echoes through the empty jail's halls. He picked Carson up and carefully maneuvered him through the gate, leaning through as far as he could so he could place Carson down again, this time by the back of his shirt. Sylas then climbed through the gate, landing feet first next to Carson. He put Carson back in the chair, and then continued to stroll him through the prison toward the main doors. When they reached the doors and walked outside, Sylas let out a loud "woohoo" and then got down on hands and knees to kiss the ground. He turned and sat on the ground, laughing. "Man, it feels good to be out here. How long you think this cloud is gonna hang around?"

Carson looked down at his feet. "I don't know," he said, again in a quiet voice. He cleared his throat and spoke louder. "My boy has a big plan. I'm sure he's got this under control."

Sylas nodded, looking impressed. "That's cool. What is his plan for you? When are we going back to Moon City?"

"We wait," Carson answered. "We just wait, for now."

Sylas looked less impressed. "For how long?"

Carson took a long look at the sky before answering. "As long as we have to."

"Well, let's find something to eat then. The mess hall was cleaned out. We gotta head into the town to look for food. The other inmates already got almost a day on us."

Carson looked at Sylas, tucked his lips and nodded. "Sylas, we're going to be fine. Eli won't leave us here. He'll come for us."

"Yeah, well he better. I've taken good care of you. He owes me." Sylas cracked his neck and adjusted his shoulders. "He may have never called you, but he better not be so ungrateful with me."

Carson looked down again. Looking up only meant looking for a ship from his son that wouldn't come. "Come on, Sylas," he said. "Let's head to town and find you something to eat."

Sylas stood, and began pushing Carson in his chair.

19

Nolan drove into Chicago in his dad's old truck wearing his dad's old clothes over his uniform. His days as Savior were on hold; he was too weak to run, let alone teleport anywhere. It felt like the atmosphere itself was trying to press him into the ground. Moving his body had become an act of violence against itself. The recent absence of his powers left him nearly useless, and attributing it to Earth's eternal night, he wallowed in his newfound deficiency. His landing on the ground and the subsequent battle with S.W.A.R.M. a few weeks back had tattooed him with pain. Nolan had never dealt with the mortality of a fragile body and it scared him.

Despite his injuries and fatigue, he was determined to reset the sky and end the darkness. The solution to the QuestCorp cloud had to be somewhere within QuestCorp. It made sense to start his search in Moon City, but first he needed to find a ride there. Getting to Moon City to look for answers meant taking a shuttle flight, and even though he wasn't sure his body could handle the gravitational forces from the ship's ascent through Earth's atmosphere, he knew there was no other option.

Entering Chicago, Nolan noticed that what was once a bright city full of life now only shone with flickering streetlamps and sporadically lighted buildings. He had set out with a plan to stake out Chicago's QuestCorp complex and then wait for the company's lunar shuttle to make a hydrogen delivery, though he wasn't certain a shuttle would even come to the complex. And even if it did, he had no idea how he would get onboard, or how he could remain there undiscovered. Earth had become a hostile, alien world to him and he had struggled to adapt. Adaptation, however, was the best he could hope to do now.

Once in the city, Nolan parked his father's truck a few blocks from the QuestCorp complex, then slowly walked the rest of the way. He looked around for a place to hide out and wait for the shuttle delivering shipments from Moon City. The streets near the complex were vacant and soulless like everything else he passed on his way to the city. The cafes and restaurants, gadget stores, and boutiques that previously thrived along the city blocks surrounding the QuestCorp hub were now all just shells of an old life. Nolan decided to set up his watch inside an empty luncheonette from which he could see the shuttle's landing area inside the QuestCorp facility.

Sitting in the empty restaurant, uncomfortable and pained, Nolan thought about how he just left his mother behind in what was now an uncertain world. She had done what she could to try and nurse his health, cooking him every recipe she had from a lifetime of feeding the world's strongest man. The constant look of worry on her face stayed with him after he left, though. Leaving her alone in this dark world was a hard choice to make, but staying so she could watch him fade was no great option either. He owed it to her to fix what had broken, or at least put up a good fight. He looked back with regret at the moment he decided to rush toward the mysterious and unnatural plume that was flooding the sky with an unknown gas. Not regret for trying to do something, but regret for not thinking it through first, and in doing so jeopardizing his ability to help. Now, people were suffering, and his powerlessness would do no one any good.

After spending a little time in the luncheonette, he decided to find a spot to hide closer to the shuttle's landing pad since he struggled so much to move even a little, and wanted to be as close as possible when it was time to act. He hadn't even crossed the street when the complex's surveillance array activated and tracked him with cameras and infrared scanners. A handful of S.W.A.R.M. robots from within the lobby of the building were synced to the camera's video feed and started moving in the direction of where Nolan was walking. Seeing S.W.A.R.M. on the move, he turned and hobbled down the sidewalk, away from the robot guards as fast as he could. As he fumbled to find an open door of a storefront to slip into, he glanced over his shoulder toward the oncoming bots. He stumbled on his feet, and something hit his head just before he blacked out.

20

When Nolan came to he had no idea where he was, other than laid out on a cold floor somewhere. A man and two women were staring at him. They looked frightened. Each held a gun aimed at him.

One of the women spoke to him. "What are you doing here?"

Nolan just looked back her, not knowing what was in store, but knowing he wouldn't be able to handle whatever it was.

The woman spoke again. "You don't look well. Are you sick? What are you doing here? You're not from QuestCorp, are you?"

Nolan tried to sit up, but the woman placed her foot on his shoulder and kicked him back to the ground. He hit his head, which reminded him that his head hurt from being struck earlier. "Stay put!" She said.

"Okay. Okay. I'm not any trouble," Nolan said. "I just need to catch my breath and then I'll leave. I don't want any trouble."

The woman continued to speak for the group. "There's no trouble here, at least not from us. We heard the S.W.A.R.M. alarm. We saw them coming out after you. You stumbled and hit your head, but we were able to get you away through these buildings. But they're still searching for you, I guarantee it."

Nolan was still trying to catch his breath, so he struggled to speak. "I heard them coming and ran. Can you lower your guns?"

"They were probably alerted by the sounds of your distress. They can detect elevated heartrate, and body temperature. Did you know that? They're designed to help people, but lately that hasn't always been the case. We didn't want give them the chance to make another potentially useful disappear, but…" the woman paused, obviously evaluating the extent of his injuries, "…who are you?"

"Do you know a lot about them?" Nolan asked.

"S.W.A.R.M.? Yeah. They're QuestCorp robotics. We work for QuestCorp."

Nolan looked at the woman with surprise. "Why are you hiding in here then?"

"It's a long story."

Nolan slowly sat up against a wall, wincing while he moved, all the while trying to ensure he didn't get kicked down again. "I've got time. I could use the moment's rest, honestly. I'm not a threat."

"I'll say," the man said, motioning for everyone to lower their guns. "You can barely move."

"I'm just waiting for a ride."

"It doesn't look like you should be riding around anywhere in your condition," the woman said. "What are you doing out here alone? Maybe you *should* risk it and let S.W.A.R.M. administer some care. They've got doctors and food inside the building. And medicine. Just don't act aggressive or even apprehensive toward them; they've been punchy lately with stuff like that."

"I don't want help from those robots. Why are *you* hiding here?"

The two women looked at the man, who paused, but finally answered Nolan's question. "We're waiting for a ride."

Nolan looked at the man curiously.

"The QuestCorp shuttle," the man said, reluctantly.

"I don't understand. You just said you work for—"

"—Eli Quest is a madman. He has been holding employees like prisoners. Here and on the Moon. He's collecting all his employees on the Moon little by little. The whole company actually."

"Why?"

The woman answered. "He's going to leave S.W.A.R.M. here on Earth to take care of people. He is going to take care of all *his* people up there."

Nolan looked at the woman, puzzled. "He's not going to fix the problem?"

"No. S.W.A.R.M. is the fix. Along with the food they make from hydrogen."

The look of confusion didn't leave Nolan's face. The other woman joined the conversation. "The problem, as you see it, isn't a problem for him. He planned all this. He planned for the cloud, and everything that followed."

"Why would he do such a thing? How do you *know* he planned it?"

"I'll answer that," the man said. "My name's Armstrong. I'm a Flight Commander for the QuestCorp lunar shuttle. This is Janet Briggs and Dawn Hutchins. QuestCorp released the cloud on purp—"

"—WHY!?"

"Keep your voice down," Armstrong said, looking out a window to make sure S.W.A.R.M. wasn't near. "I don't know. I *do* know someone close to the operation though. She filled me in. She is coming here from Moon City, so she can fix it. We're going to meet her shuttle when it lands. This isn't right, what they're doing. I didn't sign up for this."

Nolan was stuck on the news he'd just heard. "So, what is it? Some kind of gas?"

"I don't know."

"Will it go away on its own?"

"My friend says she has a plan. She needs us here to take over as shuttle crew once she lands. That's all I know. We want to fix this thing for everyone's sake; we didn't sign up for this."

Nolan sensed Armstrong's sincerity in his desire to help but didn't see how he could. "It doesn't seem like you have much of a plan."

"I'm just going on what I know."

"Well I need to get to Moon City. Can you take me there?"

Briggs interrupted. "The ride to the Moon isn't easy on the body."

"I'll be fine. Especially once I get to the Moon."

"We're waiting for the shuttle," Armstrong said. "Once we rendezvous with my friend, we go where she says we go. And I don't know if that's going to be the Moon or not. Rest, but then get out of here. Things could get messy, and you're not going to want to get caught up in it. When we make our move, you need to run. It's nothing personal."

Nolan nodded.

"Do you want something to eat?" Hutchins asked. "You look like you need to eat."

"No, thanks. Food isn't going to help."

"What's wrong with you?" She asked.

"I'll tell you, but you won't believe me. But, first, I need you to tell me how I can get to Moon City. Will another shuttle come after your friend's?"

"I just told you you'd never make the trip in your condition," Briggs answered. "And trust me, you don't want to be up there. You don't want to cross paths with Eli Quest. He's a smart man with a lot of resources."

Desperate for a way off Earth, Nolan fished for more information. "What's so bad about Eli Quest?"

"So bad?" Armstrong asked. "So Bad!? Hey, man, look around! Look what he's done! Could it be any worse? He went on TV and claimed it was some kind of corporate sabotage. But in six different facilities at the same exact time?"

Briggs looked at Armstrong sternly and raised a finger to her lips.

"A cover then?" Nolan asked. Armstrong just shook his head and looked down at the ground. Nolan continued. "This cloud is a front for something bigger?"

"What could be bigger than what is happening right now?" Hutchins asked. "Here, eat this." She threw what looked like a wrapped candy bar to Nolan.

He caught the bar and noticed it was different than any food he'd seen before. "What is this?"

"It's hydrogen-based. It doesn't taste great, but you can eat it."

"Thanks." Nolan looked that the food bar, and then put it aside.

Hutchins laughed. "Oh, man, I don't blame you. What's your name?"

"My name is Nolan. Most people call me Savior."

21

Nolan had nodded off, but woke to impassioned voices from the crew discussing the plan of reentry into the QuestCorp building, and how they would get onto the shuttle undetected. As the crew discussed their options, Nolan thought it seemed more like a negotiation of strategies than of planning. Hutchins looked over at Nolan. "Feeling any better?"

"I'm not a hundred percent."

"You need to eat."

She handed him some hydrogen-based food and a bottle of water. "It's not like it'll make you any worse."

"Thanks." Nolan unwrapped the food, took a bite and grimaced.

Hutchins laughed. "Well, yeah. It's made from the Sun. They say they're working on the flavor. It's all we have right now."

"I appreciate you sharing it with me," Nolan said, respectfully, and then tucked the food bar away.

Hutchins rejoined the discussion with Briggs and Armstrong.

"There is no way," Armstrong said. "Even *with* Savior, there is no way we can get past S.W.A.R.M. without the virus. And, he can barely walk. We need to install it again."

"I'm not sure if reinstalling it will even work," Briggs replied. "I don't know if it was designed for more than a single use, nor do I know if it will even be effective now that S.W.A.R.M. has already been exposed to it. The whole system could already be re-encrypted, or they could have programmed an immunity."

Nolan, still sitting on the floor, chimed in. "What exactly is the virus?"

"My friend on the Moon smuggled it to us," Armstrong said. "We used it to temporarily shut down S.W.A.R.M. when we left the facility."

Standing slowly to join the crew, Nolan asked another question. "Wouldn't it be designed to help you escape and meet this friend of yours?"

Briggs answered. "I installed the virus early. I didn't know it would launch automatically. I thought I'd have to press "OK" or something. Computer viruses aren't really my area of expertise. I panicked and told the team we had to go. We ran out of the complex and hid out while S.W.A.R.M. was infected. It didn't know we escaped. We were supposed to upload the virus, go to the shuttle when it landed, and take off while S.W.A.R.M. was offline. It would have worked if I hadn't tried to preload it."

Nolan nodded, understanding the issue. "So, you figure QuestCorp knows that a virus was released against S.W.A.R.M. and has taken action to counter a future attack. Things as they are, I think there is only one way to find out. When does your friend arrive?"

"The shuttle's due in tonight," Armstrong replied. "But S.W.A.R.M. security is pretty tight. After our virus fiasco, I don't know what our chances are of meeting up with her, or if the shuttle will even show."

"Not to mention they've probably looked back at surveillance tapes and identified us as the attackers," Briggs added.

"It will show," Hutchins said. "It would have left Moon City before we installed the virus. Nora should be on the shuttle, and it should land as scheduled. It won't have enough fuel to land elsewhere."

"And if it was somehow delayed?" Briggs asked.

"If it was delayed we'll know soon enough." Armstrong said. "The plan has changed a bit, but we need to make it work. We need to get into the lobby and re-install the virus on one of the computers there."

"It can't be done remotely?" Nolan asked.

Armstrong pursed his lips and looked down. "No. We left our equipment behind when we ran. This isn't exactly business-as-usual for us."

"I hear you," Nolan said, in a consolatory way. "So, you don't have the virus anymore?"

"Each of us were given a copy, just in case," Briggs said. "I left mine behind. We still have two copies."

Nolan paused, thinking for a minute. "It may just be that the four of us, and your friend, are the best chance at getting rid of this cloud. Two copies of the virus, two teams."

"We split up?" Armstrong asked. "What do you have in mind?"

22

Nolan and Armstrong looked to get into QuestCorp the same way the crew got out, through the front door. Getting into the lobby to access one of the computers at the security desk was likely going to set off S.W.A.R.M.'s alert system, but the plan was to get in and upload the virus to take S.W.A.R.M. offline before it could reach them. Without remote access to the QuestCorp mainframe, shutting it down from the lobby computer was a gamble.

The two split off from Briggs and Hutchins who set out to find an alternate entrance to the shuttle bay, if one existed. For Nolan and Armstrong, getting near the front door proved to be impossible. A S.W.A.R.M. squadron was alerted to them almost immediately once they neared the complex. It surrounded them just outside the building in a fashion honoring its namesake. A tinny voice called out commands to them: *Please state your name for voice identification processing.*

Armstrong was accustomed to the S.W.A.R.M. protocol, but it was unclear whether his status as a deserter was now logged in the robots' mainframe.

"Commander Joseph Armstrong."

Without pause, the tin voice responded. *Identity confirmed.* After a brief pause a bot leaned toward Nolan. *Please state your name for voice identification processing.*

Nolan initially didn't answer, because he was feeling different than he'd felt recently. It fascinated him, to the point of distraction. The robot repeated its request, but this time Nolan answered: "I'm Doctor Nolan Keller."

Identity not registered. Repeat for identification.

"Doctor Nolan Keller. I work on the third floor in Advanced Applied Sciences."

"Identification failed. Please provide identification badge for barcode scan."

"Sure. It's right here in my pocket. Hold on." Nolan reached toward his pocket, looking at Armstrong with apprehension. The look on his face told Nolan everything he needed to know. Likely, they would only have minutes to deal with the robot squadron before the whole legion converged on them. Nolan's muscles twitched, and he started to feel anxious though energized, but was altogether unsure if what he was feeling meant what he hoped it might.

His instincts spoke, and he listened. He motioned as if he was pulling an I.D. badge out of his pocket, and in a swift and powerful motion swung his opposing fist forward, connecting with the head unit of one of the robots, sending it flying up over the street and into a crosswalk. It shorted out before it even landed. Nolan quickly grabbed Armstrong, turned his back toward the doors of the QuestCorp main lobby and ran backward, plowing down several S.W.A.R.M. bots that were rushing out before crashing through the complex's glass doors. He let go of Armstrong so he could run and hide, or find a computer to load the virus. S.W.A.R.M. flowed into the lobby, taking an aggressive stance once again against Nolan. The posh lobby quickly turned into a battleground as fists of metal lunged toward Nolan, now feeling more like Savior again.

The walls and doorways, along with the concierge desk in the lobby, were smashed in the fight. Glass windows, the elevator doors and furniture were all destroyed as Nolan tossed robot after robot. He grabbed a hold of a one and shredded it to pieces with his bare hands, tossing its parts to the ground, just in time to get his hands up to grab hold of the next advancing metal minion. The horde came at him like waves from the sea, but somehow, he stood his ground. He exchanged punch after punch with a tidal wave of robot fists. With no sign of slowing from either side, it looked as though the building around them would crumble before a victor was decided. Realizing the danger, Nolan yelled to Armstrong to evacuate, but when he attempted to run through the remnants of the lobby along the edge of the battle, he was snatched mid-stride by S.W.A.R.M., which immediately ceased its aggression toward Nolan, who was starting to show signs of fatigue. He stopped pushing against the robots once he saw his new friend struggling against S.W.A.R.M. as it held him by his neck. Nolan exhaled and slumped his shoulders, sinking to the floor in what had quickly become a total defeat. He didn't want to see Armstrong hurt, and the burst of strength he had experienced had faded in the fight.

S.W.A.R.M. issued a warning to Nolan. *"Continued violence will result in the elimination of QuestCorp personnel Joseph Armstrong. Stand down if you do not wish to cause harm. This will be your only warning."*

"I stand down. Don't hurt him."

There was no way Nolan could determine a robot's bluff. He surrendered, and Armstrong was ushered away. Once again S.W.A.R.M. surrounded Nolan in an uncomfortably tight circle. Grabbing hold of his arms and legs, S.W.A.R.M. swung him around so that he was facing the now destroyed entrance to the building. Through the piles of rubble and broken glass, a man carrying a large, unusual gun walked into the lobby, and then proceeded directly to where Nolan was being held. The man sized him up and expressed a look of indignation. He looked at the destroyed lobby and shook his head in disdain.

"I am Eli Quest," he said. "Welcome to QuestCorp. You work for me now, Savior."

23

Eli rested his hand on his big gun, which was propped up on his desk and aimed at Nolan's heart. He spoke in a civil, matter-of-fact way. "Frankly, I am surprised you haven't been torn apart yet, and that you managed to escape death at the hands of S.W.A.R.M. twice. You truly are something, Nolan, but you are in no way a hero. Not today anyway."

"Sorry to disappoint."

Eli's lips pursed while his brow and jaw locked in a way that trumpeted hatred from within. The fact that Nolan would not go quietly into the night was a part of his plan that remained unchecked.

"Disappoint?" Eli let out a quick burst of laughter. "You haven't disappointed me. Maybe all your fans out there, maybe everyone quivering in the dark, suffering through their fears in the absence of their Sun and 'hero.' But no, you haven't disappointed me, Nolan. To me you are just a meddlesome alien. An invasive species trying to overtake the natural order of things. I know you. All your powers, all the secrets from your ship. You're not one of us. Getting rid of you was supposed to be folded within my larger plan, but you've proven to be more capable in the face of certain death than I had estimated. My only disappointment is in myself, and the fact that I haven't finished the job yet. But, since you are here, I have something else in mind."

"I've never caused harm to you, or anything you've done with your company, yet you built a robot army to try and kill me? Armies have tried to destroy me before, yet here I am. You overestimate yourself."

Eli scoffed. "Oh, I've done more than just build an army. S.W.A.R.M. wasn't created to kill you, though it could. The death of Earth will be the death of you." Eli smiled before he could get the rest of his words out. "The only thing I overestimated was how quickly my cloud would crush you. But it is just a matter of time."

"You're a madman."

"I am a *hero*, Nolan Keller. *I* am the world's savior. Everyone will soon look up to *me*! I created a final solution for the human race that will usher in a new and lasting era of peace and prosperity. I gave the world all the power and food it needs; made sure that every person on the planet could have a full belly and a warm place to sleep at night. I reached out to mankind and lent it a hand, which did more than anyone like you could ever dream of doing. Other than stopping tanks and zapping yourself here and there to save a few unfortunate souls, what have you done for mankind? Absolutely nothing but disrupt the natural order of things, saving the weak so that they can thrive in the face of those who are stronger, those *truly* meant to survive." Eli leaned back in his chair, a look of pure contempt permanently holding on his face. "You've been on this planet for less than half a century, yet you feel you have the right to interfere. Mankind has battled itself for millennia, and then you come along and think you can play God, deciding for yourself who lives and dies. That's not how it works. Mankind is a pure race. It cleanses *itself* as it moves forward. We have evolved over millions of years without you to get us where we are. You have *no* right to interfere."

"What are you talking about, I—"

"—I'm talking about *you*, Savior. You are an unnatural influence. You are a disease and like a disease you must be eradicated. Mankind doesn't need you, and soon they will see this."

"This cloud you unleashed will kill the planet and starve mankind unless they eat food you engineered from atoms, and you think *I* am the unnatural influence?!"

Eli gave Nolan a cold stare, then looked at the massive gun aimed at Nolan's chest. "You see this gun? It's a plasma cannon. It's loaded with an ionized element discovered lodged in *your* ship. My father actually found it. You probably have heard of my father, he's the guy who—"

"—I know who your father is."

Eli smiled. "Of course. Well, just like you, I was never able to stop him from doing whatever he wanted to do either, which was usually chasing after one lost cause or another. But when he discovered your ship, well, that was one he got right."

"You're a murder just like your father, only you're worse; you are a world killer. So, shoot me, or am I just supposed to be scared by your gun?

Eli looked at Nolan with a feigned amusement that masked his contempt. "Have patience. I'll get to that. But, enough about my father, let's talk about yours."

Nolan stood on his feet. "I will tear off your arms and wear your—"

"—Sit down." Eli stood as well, clutching the plasma cannon with two hands. The gun began to hum quietly. "I'm not talking about Frank Keller. I'm talking about your biological father."

Nolan sat down as looks of confusion and skepticism merged on his face. Eli continued.

"Do you know anything about the cloud out there covering the Earth?" He didn't wait for Nolan to answer. "It's actually made of the same stuff that's in this gun, which is an ionized element from another galaxy. I've named it Elijum; I think the name rolls off the tongue. Our forensic investigation suggested that crystals we found penetrating the hull of your ship weren't part of the ship's intended payload. It's more than likely they collided with your ship somewhere along your journey to Earth. Regardless, we spent a lot of time and money studying the Elijum, and it paid off. It's very useful stuff. Want to see what it does up close?" Eli smiled as Nolan just stared back coldly. Eli continued. "We found a second type of crystal in your ship as well. This one was clear and sculpted; about as large as my fist. At first, we thought it was a precious stone from whatever world the ship came from, but when we ran it through testing we discovered it is actually a computer. It activates when exposed to relics from your home world. It turns out it was your father's computer, a scientist who studied the death of your planet. He catalogued a great deal of it. There is a lot of video data that shows the last days of your planet, as well as his life. There are also a lot of files on the computer that we can't understand; language and writing that is just too alien to decode. I'd like you to take a look and see if any of it makes sense."

Nolan glared at Eli, saying nothing. Eli kept speaking. "The Elijum that made the cloud, as well as what is in this gun, has been bombarded with radiation, something we synthesized after discovering its source on your ship. It's a nasty little cocktail, but only immediately lethal to you. I did have a shield installed at all my facilities to deflect the effects, however. It is radiation after all. That's why you regained your strength. As long as you are in my facility you will stave off death. So, since you haven't died, I want you to take a look at your father's work."

"I'm not here to help you."

"Well then why are you here? Helping is what you do, right?"

Nolan stared at Eli, boiling silently.

Eli dug in. "You know, we learned the benefits of Elijum from your mother. Your real mother, that is. Well, her remains anyway. What we've learned is that in a short period of time, the right level of exposure to this radioactive Elijum will degrade you on a cellular level. Anyway, that's what happened to her bones when we exposed them to it."

"My mother—"

"—what?! What?! Your mother what? You don't even know. Her bone cells resembled that of a plant's more than anything else. Her cellular walls had strength never before seen in cellular biology, even in the state of decay they were in. I can only assume that's where your tremendous strength comes from. However, exposed to the radioactive Elijum found in your ship, her bones released an enzyme that could dissolve flesh as a self-preservation instinct. It's a pretty disgusting trait, in my opinion."

Nolan stood up and lunged toward Eli. Eli stood and moved away, backing up against the windows behind him. He aimed his gun at Nolan and put his finger on the trigger.

"Relax! Just relax. Your birth mother is gone, but Mariel Keller isn't. I have positioned S.W.A.R.M. very near to her, and she'll be paid a visit unless I say otherwise. Same goes for your pilot friend, so get a hold of yourself."

Nolan looked at Eli with a swell of rage in his eyes so great that they began to darken. "I'll kill you!"

"I'm not bluffing. I can give the kill command right now." He held his watch up to his mouth. The dark rage in Nolan's eyes intensified. Eli adjusted the gun to a mild setting and then squeezed the trigger, shooting Nolan in the chest. Nolan's breath was knocked out of him as he fell back and down, hitting the ground with a grunt. Laid out, he was hard pressed to move even a finger. Eli walked over to him and bent down, getting in his face.

"I just want you to have a look at some data. Don't get so bent out of shape."

Nolan struggled, but managed to get a few words out. "Don't hurt her."

Eli stood up and looked down at Nolan. "I will say that it pains me slightly to enlist your aid, but step out of line again and the next shot I fire won't be at you, and it won't be from a plasma gun."

"Don't."

Eli smiled, and leaned in even closer to Nolan's face. "All the power you possess can't save the human race from what lies ahead. I am their savior now."

24

When Nora exited the shuttle with Arthur Chance, Edward and Elena, she expected to be greeted by Joe Armstrong and his crew. Instead, she was greeted by Eli, his devilish smile, and a squadron of his robots. She and the scientists were escorted separately by S.W.A.R.M. into the QuestCorp facility as Eli followed. Each were taken to different parts of the building. Eli stayed with Nora as she was ushered to a small office and sat in a chair at a table. S.W.A.R.M. lined the walls all around her as Eli sat down in the chair next to her.

"Hello, Nora. Did you think I didn't know you left Moon City?" Nora looked away from Eli. He feigned amusement. "You did. I see. Well, it's nice to see you. You have quite a talent for getting caught though. If S.W.A.R.M. wasn't just a program housed by circuits and bolts, I'd say it was probably getting bored having to constantly retrieve you."

"Don't be an asshole."

Eli smiled. "Don't be an asshole. Don't be a…you know what…how about *you* don't plot behind my back and *you* don't betray me? You cannot best me, no matter what you think you know."

"Eli, you need to stop what you are doing. You need to undo this insanity."

Eli smiled again, his eyes fixed on Nora. "Stop? There is no stop. What is done can't be undone. Your little attempt at a revolt was precious. I can appreciate passion, and I can't fault you for your ignorance. Edward and the others, however, they should all know better. It's their science. They designed this destruction. They haven't told you the cloud is irreversible?"

"If we can't stop you, why are you here to stop us? You hate Earth."

Eli laughed and stood from his chair, walking along the ranks of S.W.A.R.M. robots flanking the room. "The last place I want to be is on the planet, but work is work. I won't tolerate this insubordination from my employees. I am not here to stop you; you haven't started anything. I'm here to bring you home. Earth is a dangerous place now, and it has nothing left to offer you. You're coming back to Moon City with me until it's time to leave. On our new world you, and everyone else, will have so much more. You will see, and sooner than you think. We make a good team, and frankly I don't want any deficiencies in my operation once we transition."

Nora shook her head. "That's all you care about."

"THERE IS NOTHING ELSE! I am personally delivering mankind its best chance. Everything else along the way is inconsequential. I want you by my side, and I want those scientists to continue their scientific advancements, but if you think for a minute that I will tolerate resistance then you are not the intelligent woman I credit you to be."

"You're crazy!" Rage and tears poured out of her. "You are insane if you think this is okay! You've killed everything, and you think it is okay! What happened to you? What made you do this? What made you think—"

"—ENOUGH! I won't be questioned. This is what's right, and necessary. We will all die here one day if we don't move on. I am doing what needs to be done. Anything lost along the way will only make us stronger in the end. I know what's best."

Nora sat speechless, confounded by Eli's insistence on ending the world only to start a new one.

He sat down next to her again. "What were you were planning, Nora? What were you trying to accomplish by bringing the scientists to Earth?"

Nora shook, trying to gain composure, but let the fight in her do the talking. She swung her hand at Eli, who deflected it with his forearm. He balled up his fist and slammed it down on the table in front of her. She jumped up from her chair, but Eli wrenched her back into her seat by her arm. He then stood, not breaking eye contact. "Fight all you want. You will not win." He turned away from her, giving orders to S.W.A.R.M. as he left the room. "Keep her on Earth. Send her and the scientists with the other prisoners, and double security once they all arrive. Get my jet ready."

He looked back to Nora. "Earth is dead. Whatever you thought you could gain by coming back to it was just foolish thought. See for yourself what life now means on this planet. You'll wish you'd stayed in Moon City soon enough."

25

Eli sat alone in a control room in his facility in central Europe, which was Earth's headquarters for the Demeter Initiative. He had arrived only minutes earlier from Chicago. It was nothing like his office in Moon City but provided a more centralized command for a plan that was showing some loose ends. The control room was lined with video monitors that showed an array of information, and Eli was busy scouring them all. Since this facility was the most secure on Earth he had S.W.A.R.M. deposit Nolan and Armstrong, Nora, and the scientists in it. He could see each of them being led to holding rooms on the monitors, as well as the live feeds from several S.W.A.R.M. squadrons. Each squadron was rounding up people from all over the globe and relocating them to a refugee center set up outside the facility. Despite the destruction of Earth, the decline of civilization, the looming extinction of the human race, and the betrayal of his most trusted employees, he saw the current state of the world as the final minutes before his finest hour. The hour in which he would prove beyond doubt that the human race was an unstoppable machine, naturally selected through the most painful events to transcend limitation. His eyes were fixed on the screens as spoke into his watch.

"Bring me Arthur Chance."

"Affirmative."

As Eli waited for Arthur, he watched an endless line of people being escorted into the tent city just outside the facility, watching as they walked past posters of beautiful sunlit meadows and pristine lakes displayed along the path, as well as televisions broadcasting messages of QuestCorp's devotion to a brighter future, as they slowly shuffled in. They were being staged for the final phase of his vision.

S.W.A.R.M. finally entered the control room with Arthur.

Eli greeted him enthusiastically. "Last Chance! Welcome to the liberation of mankind."

S.W.A.R.M. pushed Arthur down into a chair. He shook his head and rolled his eyes. Eli cut to the point. "I would like an update on the wormhole cache."

Arthur glared at the robots before answering Eli. "What exactly do you want to know? Is it still locked? Yes. Have I figured out what the hell is in there that turned Wu inside out? No. It's in the goddamn fourth dimension, Eli. We will never know what happened. Opening it again would be a mistake."

Eli rubbed his chin while he stared at Arthur. "That's not what I wanted to hear. Not at all. Look here, Arthur." Eli pointed to the to monitor showing the inpouring of refugees. "These people are ready for their new home. They are counting on you to help get them there. I want a wormhole open to the new planet. Now."

"That's not going to happen."

"Why?"

"Why? Wu, that's why. You run the risk of what happened to him also happening to everyone you send across the bridge into the wormhole cache."

"Then open a new wormhole in our dimension. Forget the cache."

"You can't do that either."

Eli's brow furrowed. "Why not?"

"You already have a wormhole created in the cache to the new planet. You can't open another one at the same coordinates. There is no model for doing that. Two overlaying folds of the space-time continuum? I have no idea what could happen, and after Wu, well, I wouldn't take any more chances."

Eli glanced at a monitor. It showed Edward being placed into a secure room. "What does Edward think?"

"Edward caused this whole problem. Who cares what Edward thinks?"

"I do. What is his plan? He knows what we are up against. The wormholes are his passion. Why did you come to Earth with him?

"Nora said you wanted us all here."

Eli gritted his teeth. "Arthur, you have a choice. Open the wormhole cache and access the wormhole we need, or you and Edward can reestablish a new one. I don't care about the original. I don't care what weird science comes out of this mess. We can leave it all behind us when we travel to our new home because we won't be coming back here."

Arthur looked at Eli smugly. "I'm not doing anything."

"Let me rephrase it then. Give me my wormhole or become a casualty for the cause."

"No, Eli. You can't scare me into doing this. The unknown of what you are asking is way scarier. There is no way of knowing what other dangers we will create, and on what scale, if we act rashly. We're talking about a possible monumental catastrophe!"

"I'm all for destroying the connection to the fourth dimension and the cache after we get where we need to go."

"We can't go where we need to go without opening it, and I'm not opening it."

Eli's face tightened with frustration, but then quickly relaxed. "Arthur. I want to help you better understand the choice you are making. I trust you to accomplish what needs to be done more than anyone else right now. Wu told me what is on the other side. It's a creature, a four dimensional being of some kind. According to Wu, it's incomprehensible, but it's there. Inserting the cache into its dimension likely caused its aggression. It's within reason that extracting the cache will rectify the situation. Wu was rambling on about it in his coma, and still goes on about it now that he's awake. It scared him beyond reckoning, but I believe *you* can fix this. We still have a job to do. You have an opportunity to stabilize everything, you just have to take the chance."

Arthur shook his head. "Ask someone else."

Eli clenched his fists and furled his lips. He couldn't afford to get rid of Arthur but wasn't going to get anywhere with him either. "Because of everything you have done for me over the years, I am going to let you sleep on it. Your answer better be 'Yes' in the morning, though."

Arthur stared at Eli before standing up and walking out of the control room. "I'll see myself out," he said, taking his time. Arthur knew how to languish on Eli's last nerve. As he passed through the door and turned down the hall, S.W.A.R.M. closed ranks behind him and escorted him away.

Eli glanced at a monitor on the wall displaying Nora's quarters. He then spoke into his watch. "Any word?"

A synthetic voice responded. *"Negative. No information from Nora Reinhard."*

"Sync with the other squadrons. Give her some space. See if she says anything when she encounters the others."

"Affirmative. Syncing. Sync complete. Releasing Nora Reinhard."

Eli looked down at the floor, his hand on his chin. S.W.A.R.M. was good at finding things, and if Nora had a plan to stop him, it was a plan he needed to know. He just had to wait for her to slip and divulge it to someone.

"Maintain surveillance. High priority," he said to the robot battalion.

"Affirmative."

Eli stared at Nora in the monitor. "What are you up to?"

26

Nora was outside the QuestCorp facility, walking alone along the wall that separated it from the refugee camp on the other side. S.W.A.R.M. trailed not far behind. As she walked, she could hear the televisions on the other side broadcasting a news report to the refugees.

"Good evening. I'm Emilia Trust, and you're watching the 'QuestCorp Daily Report' podcast. Tonight, we take another look at events in Europe, where great efforts have recently been made by Eli Quest and QuestCorp to end what has been a progressively violent conflict surrounding a QuestCorp food distribution center between citizens and S.W.A.R.M., the automated relief system of robots originally created by QuestCorp to serve as aid workers, now doubling as enforcer of law and order. While groups of hungry people as well as organized bands of raiders from the growing refugee center have somewhat routinely attempted to breach the QuestCorp operations facilities, a new approach to law enforcement has been unveiled by the company, which is working hard to hold humanity together during its darkest times. Savior, once the world's greatest symbol of hope and humanity, has recently shown up at the company's European hub after an unexplained absence from the world, and will be joining S.W.A.R.M. in standing guard. Video footage from the QuestCorp archives have shown Savior standing atop the security wall keeping a watchful eye for any of the desperate marauders, helping S.W.A.R.M. protect the QuestCorp operation that is feeding and caring for all of humanity. Since his arrival a few days ago there have been no reported attacks or attempts to break into the QuestCorp facilities, and the company is hoping that with Savior now on the job, conflict within the refugee center will decrease.

There are many questions here that need answering: Where has Savior been all this time? What has he been doing? And why has he finally decided to come into the spotlight in what appears to be a partnership with QuestCorp? Yesterday, Eli Quest released a video showing him and Savior standing side by side, shaking hands, talking about how they were looking forward to sorting out the issues QuestCorp faces in western Europe, as well as feeding and housing refugees. With the world in dire straits, a new hope has begun to surge, stemming from the re-emergence of the greatest hero the world has ever known.

When asked, people within the affected camp had a mix of emotions on the subject, some saying that if Savior could have done something to fix the world's problems he'd have done it already, while others expressed joy and relief to have Savior back.

We wanted to interview both Eli Quest and Savior for this broadcast, but a spokesperson for the QuestCorp company said that both men were very busy with their tasks at hand, but were very excited for what this new partnership has in store. For now, Savior can be observed doing his duties, serving as a silent sentinel overlooking the dark horizon, sometimes taking breaks to visit people in the refugee camp, often eating with them, and helping hand out food rations. It is a sight far removed from seeing the 'World's Mightiest Man' in action, but one that this reporter welcomes as a small light of hope within these dark days.

But, even in this glimmering hope, I have to ask, now that the world as we knew it is gone, and as we, humanity, list into the night, why? In so many ways, why? Why after the Sun has gone and the flowers and trees have died alongside the wild animals, is Savior helping hand out food to a world now troubled with starvation, violence, and sickness? Why isn't he being our Savior? The answer is clear, and it's that he can't be. Whatever life is left, whatever fate lies ahead for humanity, it now lies with QuestCorp. I'm Emilia Trust, thanks for watching, and goodnight."

The report ended, and Nora let out a primal scream. "Is that the bullshit you're selling?" She shouted into the air. "Nice touch getting Emilia Trust to sell your lies!" She walked up to one of the S.W.A.R.M. robots following her and shoved her finger in its face. "You won't pull it off, Eli! You're not great enough! You're no one's hero!"

S.W.A.R.M. grabbed her and carried her away from the wall.

27

Nolan stood on the wall surrounding the QuestCorp facility alongside S.W.A.R.M. A second unit was passing below them, escorting refugees into the tented camp, which now circled the facility for miles. Nolan split his days between working with his father's computer and standing post on the wall, noting how the camp grew daily. Since he started serving as a guard, S.W.A.R.M. hadn't needed to use any lethal force against refugees trying to overtake the QuestCorp buildings.

The new status quo for Earth was survival, and for everyone, that meant merely staying alive. By working for Eli, Nolan managed to secure that for himself, as well as for his mother. His health had stabilized, which was a benefit of the radiation shield that protected the QuestCorp facility from the cloud. His newly returned abilities idled, however, as did the plan to somehow save the world from its peril. Watching the darkness from the wall for an attack that never came gave Nolan a chance to observe S.W.A.R.M. up close, but it was otherwise utterly boring. There wasn't much to see, which made it easy to see everything.

Looking down from the top of the wall, he noticed a figure in the camp obscured in heavy robes a short distance away. It stood motionless, statuesque, no hint of the person under the robes ever showing. The figure only cultivated intrigue within Nolan, a man who had nothing, or very little, to fear.

After a quick side-to-side glance at the S.W.A.R.M. robots on the wall alongside him, Nolan began to charge with electricity and instantly teleported himself to the figure which was less than a hundred yards away. As he reappeared before the figure, he heard S.W.A.R.M. begin to mobilize. He looked at the figure, still obscured by the heavy robes, accept for a hand, raised, holding out an apple. Nolan was confused. With S.W.A.R.M. approaching, the figure retreated into the crowded rows of tents. Nolan turned just in time to see S.W.A.R.M. surrounding him. He put his hands in the air but was immediately struck down by a blast from an Elijum cannon. As he laid on the ground, weak from the blast, a crowd of refugees gathered. S.W.A.R.M. instantly began knocking them down and back. A fight broke out between man and machine as Nolan's vision blurred before he blacked out.

28

Nolan woke to Eli's annoyed face staring down at him. "I thought we had an understanding," he said. "Try something like that again and I will forget my side of the deal."

Nolan was weak and groggy. He tried to speak, but nothing coherent came out.

"You caused a riot. The people out there thought S.W.A.R.M. killed you. It is still working to quell the fighting as we speak. I had you dragged inside so you could revive yourself. As soon as you can make any sense, you're going on camera and telling everyone to rest at ease."

Nolan tried to speak again but was still too dazed from the ion blast.

"It's strong stuff," Eli said. "Elijum can easily kill you with the right dose. I need you to remember that. For the time being, I am going to keep you off the wall, and under guard. The two S.W.A.R.M. bots behind you are armed with that lovely little Elijum cannon."

Nolan looked behind himself and saw the two robots, noticing a man sitting in the room as well. Eli continued.

"While you are here, you need to be useful. If not, double dose. Understand? This is Edward. He is going to work with you. The robots have a gun that can settle him as well, so keep that in mind also. Edward is going to fill you in on what we already know about your father's crystal. So far, your results alone have been unimpressive. Have fun getting to know one another, and remember, I am watching. I am *always* watching." Eli pointed at S.W.A.R.M. as he spoke, then left the room.

Nolan tried to sit up, and Edward rushed over to help. He put a hand on Nolan's back to help him into a sitting position. "Sorry to be meeting you this way."

Nolan slumped forward and coughed violently. After a pause and some deep breaths, he responded. "Likewise."

"I'm Edward. I'm a physicist."

Nolan still struggled to get his words out. "Nolan. Keller."

"Right, I know who you are, Savior. It's an honor to meet you."

Before Nolan could answer, the two S.W.A.R.M. bots picked him up off the ground and sat him in a chair directly in front of a camera. *"Nolan Keller is active,"* it announced. A monitor next to the camera switched on, and Eli appeared.

"You rebounded faster than I expected. When the green light turns on, look directly into the camera, and tell everyone you are alright."

A green light on the camera blinked on. Nolan spoke. "I am okay. Please, everyone be calm."

The green light turned off, and Eli spoke through the monitor screen again. *"Good. S.W.A.R.M., broadcast immediately."*

The S.W.A.R.M. bots in the room both responded, *"Affirmative."*

Eli spoke to Edward next. *"Edward, I want you working with him nonstop on the crystal. Maybe together you can decipher the language."*

"Yes, sir."

The monitor turned off. Edward turned to Nolan. "Well, have a rest, I guess, and then we'll get started when you are up to it. Can I get you anything?"

"What do you know about the crystal?" Nolan said groggily, still dealing with the effects of the Elijum blast.

"Oh, sure. Well, where to begin. It's a bit of a long story. You see, I am part of a team that is sort of responsible for everything that is going on right now, which is also kind of all about you."

Nolan apprehensively nodded.

Edward continued. "Right, so I work for Eli. So does my wife, Elena, along with some other fellows, who all designed and managed the QuestCorp wormholes. We also got to explore a lot of those wormholes, and everything we did or discovered is all, more or less, because of what we were able to learn from reverse engineering the spaceship that brought you to Earth, as well as from the crystal."

Nolan looked at Edward with a more steadfast gaze. "Eli told me all of this. He wants to elevate mankind and I am going to be collateral damage. Deciphering the crystal will be my last contribution to the people of Earth."

Edward, surprised, continued. "Uh, right. Well, there is a lot of data on the computer. A lot has been useful, and a lot still needs to be understood. We are hoping that you might be able to help decode the language of your home world."

Nolan sighed. "I can't help you, Doctor. I was born here on Earth. I don't know anything about my home world, or my biological parents. I grew up on a farm in Denton."

"Yes, of course. I understand. But, it's still worth your time. There is a lot you can see and learn without understanding anything. A lot about where you came from. And, about your parents. You can see them in the footage, Nolan. It's worth a look." Edward paused and looked at Nolan, who had closed his eyes and was trying to get comfortable. Edward, uneasy in the silence, continued. "I'm truly sorry. I don't mean to treat this subject with insensitivity, it's just that there is a lot we can learn from this data and we are sort of down to the wire. Look, I am very responsible for all that is happening right now, and I very much want to find a way to fix things. Now, I have ideas, long shots, and I'll give them my best if that's all I've got. But, if there is something on this computer that proves to be a better idea, I need to know."

Nolan stopped trying to get comfortable and looked at Edward. "What is it that you have done, exactly, and how do you think you can fix it?"

"We've had tremendous opportunities to explore the universe. Creating the ability to grasp, at will, any and all parts of the known and unknown universe has wielded limitless potential for Eli and his company, from which he quickly drew the conclusion that the human race was short changed here on Earth. He quickly set a course to exploit the universe's resources on a quest to make mankind a superior force in the cosmos. Motivating the world to get on board was part of that plan."

"He destroyed it so that there would be no option for the people other than the one he imposed upon them," Nolan said.

"Yes, and his insurance plan was to kill you as well so that there wouldn't be anyone to stop him."

Nolan glanced at the S.W.A.R.M. robots standing like sentinels near the door. "I'm guessing Eli supports you discussing all of this with me."

"He knows that if we work together it will be for the greater good. I can't be anything but transparent and he knows that."

Nolan paused. "I can't keep a world from dying."

"Maybe not, but you can at least try. People look to you for hope. I need any help I can get to right the course."

"So, he wants to move the entire human race off Earth?"

"Yes. Well, to a new planet, more precisely, but yes."

"How?"

"Through a wormhole, which we currently can't access."

"Why not?"

"This is where this all comes together. We sort of mixed things up a bit with another dimension, and now we have problems accessing the wormholes we created."

"Why not fix Earth then? Why not lift the cloud or something?"

"I want to. I just don't know how. It's designed to be irreversible. I'm hoping something in the computer might show us how, because there is information about the materials we used to create the cloud in your father's files. We need to find a solution to all this."

Nolan shook his head. "What if there is no solution?"

"There is nothing else to go on. If your father's computer doesn't have any answers, then the alternative is searching the universe for a solution and that also requires the wormholes. I won't except a refugee camp and robot relief force as mankind's final fate, and Moon City can't support the whole population, even a reduced one. Not yet, anyway."

There was a pause in the conversation before Edward spoke again, earnestly.

"I have the workings of a plan to fix it all, Nolan. To make everything in the world right again. It's a theory, really, but if I am right it will work."

"Doctor, I want to help, but I don't think I can."

Edward leaned in close to Nolan and whispered. "I don't need you to zap yourself all over the place or be strong. Nothing spectacular like that. I just need you to try and help me understand some data. And then come to Moon City with me."

Nolan's raised his brow. "Excuse me?"

Edward glanced at the S.W.A.R.M. robots, and then continued in a whisper. "I believe the answer is in your father's computer, however, I also believe that what we are looking for to fix things is in the galaxy from which he came. In Moon City we can board the solar sailing ship to Venus to—"

"—Venus?"

"Shhh." Edward looked at S.W.A.R.M. again. The robots stood motionless. He leaned toward Nolan even more. "Yes. Venus is where we access the wormholes."

"Doctor, you just finished telling me that you can't access the wormholes."

"Yes, currently, we can't. But, now we have you. That changes everything. Once we get to Venus you may need to zap around and be strong a bit, in order to help us regain access to the wormholes there."

Nolan gave Edward a look loaded with skepticism. "How certain are you that you can find a solution once you can access your wormholes again?"

"I am not certain at all. Not yet."

Nolan shook his head, confused. "How am I supposed to help once we have reached the wormhole?"

"To best understand the answer to that question, you need to meet my friend, Chris Wu, who's in Moon City."

"Moon City again. I thought that getting to Moon City would lead me to the answer for fixing this mess, but after speaking with you, Doctor, now I'm not so sure. You seem to know a lot about what is happening, but listening to you, I can't help but think you really have no idea what you are doing."

Edward's eyes widened, and his head lurched back in disbelief. "Maybe you simply can't understand what is happening, Nolan."

"Maybe. But you make as much sense to me as this crystal. I think I'll take you up on that rest now. Let's get to work in an hour."

29

Nolan was working on his father's computer at a desk in the research lab he now shared with Edward, who had fallen asleep a few hours earlier. They had been working together for days, and Nolan was fully recovered from the Elijum ion blast. S.W.A.R.M. bots stood at the door. He was replaying one segment from the footage archive over and over. It was the last entry in the crystal's data storage, and it was about his parents, Basto and Sayla. Nolan watched the footage in silence.

Basto and Sayla laid on a bed together. Sayla looked very pregnant, and a small, empty bassinet sat just off the side of the bed. Behind them were large windows overlooking their city on their planet, Oua. It was a lush, green city, with white buildings that resembled pyramid temples, and no roadways. Aerial drone transports were moving people between buildings. In the sky hung a large green planet, a gas giant like Jupiter, hovering so close that it dominated the sky. As they rested sweetly, green glimmers of light began to appear in the distant sky. They quickly began to trail and burn as they entered the planet's atmosphere racing toward the ground. Meteor strikes began to bombard the city behind them, shaking their building, and everything around them.

The two jumped from the bed and witnessed the meteors relentlessly hammer the city. Basto grabbed Sayla by the hand, and together they ran out of the room, knocking the bassinet over as they fled. He yelled a few words causing his computer to levitate and follow. They raced out of the building and onto a large platform from which a clear tube stretched upward into the sky beyond view. A small vehicle shaped like a torpedo sat at its base, pointing upward inside it. The two got into the vehicle, and as soon as the tube sealed around it, it launched with tremendous speed. As their elevation increased, they passed multiple sections that had large gas filled balloons attached which created a ring shape around the tube. Similar tubes and rings could be seen in the distance transporting other Ouans off the planet's surface. Some had already been destroyed by the meteors.

When they reached the upper atmosphere of the planet the torpedo-shaped vehicle pushed through a soft lock at the end of the tube with great force, immediately connecting with a ring-shaped harness loaded with rocket engines. The engines ignited as soon as the vehicle locked in, automatically blasting them into space. As they left the atmosphere they saw how the meteors affected the entire planet, and how they originated from the green gas-giant's numerous moons, which were disintegrating.

The vessel docked with a space station, and Basto and Sayla were immediately out and running down a corridor lined with windows toward a cache of escape vessels primed for evacuation. As they ran down the corridor, they saw a massive rift forming on Oua below. Their sun's gravity had dragged the gas giant into Oua's orbit, resulting in Oua being torn apart by the orbital decay. They paused to look, shocked as they saw the rift split the planet into two separate pieces. A massive wave of energy shot out from the fissure, sending a powerful ripple through space that hit the space station, shaking it violently, as it shot out in all directions. Debris flew everywhere inside the station, some landing on Basto, pinning him to the floor. Sayla was knocked over, but quickly got back to her feet. Desperately, she tried to free her husband from under the debris, but she wasn't strong enough. The space station shook violently again. Basto grabbed Sayla by the hand and reassigned his computer to her by placing her thumb on its surface. Tears streamed down her face as she backed away into an escape vessel, all the while not breaking eye contact with her husband. Gently, she placed her hand on her belly, then raised her other hand to the launch button on the wall and pushed it. The small spacecraft left the station just as it broke apart.

The ship began an automated sequence to create a hyperspace passage out of the solar system, but as it entered the passage it was struck on the hull by a large piece of debris cast out from their now destroyed world. Although the spacecraft was damaged, the autopilot system was still able to navigate it through hyperspace.

The vessel soon exited hyperspace and entered Earth's atmosphere. Unbalanced by the debris lodged in the hull, the ship could not steer itself against the planet's gravity and crashed into a field on the surface. It tumbled violently as it broke into pieces, leaving a debris field in its wake. When it finally came to rest, Sayla was lying within the wreckage, badly injured, but breathing.

"How's the work coming?" Edward asked, oblivious to what Nolan was viewing.

Nolan shut down the crystal. "Good," he answered, clearing his throat. "I can't yet see what good I can do with any of this, but there is a lot to see. It's quite an education." He kept himself turned away from Edward as he spoke.

"That's putting it lightly." Edward sat down next to Nolan. "What are you viewing?"

Nolan showed Edward the crystal. "Where exactly is Oua? How far away?"

"It was about six hundred million light years away, which is nearly unfathomable without wormhole technology."

"Wow." Nolan feigned amazement. "And a wormhole allows for instant travel from there to here?"

"It does. Wormholes and hyperspace can."

"I don't understand the difference."

Edward smiled. "Think of the universe as a sheet of paper." He grabbed paper from the desk and folded two edges over each other. "A wormhole is created when you manipulate space-time and connect two points of the universe at the same location. You sort of create a momentary four-dimensional continuum, the fourth dimension being time. Hyperspace is travel through the actual, or spatial, fourth dimension. From within that dimension you can connect to our dimension at any point."

"How do you access the fourth dimension in order to do that?"

"Well, your ship taught us how to do that, and from there we were also able to derive a method for wormhole creation. It's really remarkable all the things you brought to us, Nolan. There are things we can do now that we'd be a century away from if it weren't for your technology."

Nolan looked sternly at Edward. "All this trouble the world is in wouldn't be happening either."

Edward cleared his throat nervously. "Right, well, there is that. So, what can you say you've discovered, if anything, from the crystal?"

"Honestly, I watched my world and family get torn apart."

"I'm sorry…"

"It's alright. It's something I should know. And, it's something I don't want to see repeated. Things here on Earth are bad. What is most important is preserving life and keeping families together. I know you believe there is a fix for this world, but the priority should be preservation of the human race."

"What are you saying, Nolan?"

"I'm saying we need to follow Eli's plan. We need to get everyone on this planet to the new one. Saving Earth can come later, if at all."

Edward sat, shocked. Then he looked at the door where S.W.A.R.M. was standing guard and leaned in to speak to Nolan.

"Are you serious?" He whispered. "We have to save Earth. It's the right thing to do!"

"Right or wrong, the people come first. My planet died, and I am the only one left from it. That can't happen here. Let's get Eli's wormhole running."

"We can't. I mean, it's operational, but it isn't safe at all."

"Like you said before; you have me now. How do we get to it?"

Edward's eyes widened as he took in what Nolan was saying. He glanced at S.W.A.R.M. again, standing motionless at the door, before he spoke. "A ship. The solar sailing ship, precisely. It's docked in Moon City."

"Then we go to Moon City."

"Right, okay then, if we manage to gain access to the wormhole cache, we can also use it to search for a solution for the cloud."

"Edward, first the people. Then you can save the planet. I can't be any clearer about that."

Edward rolled his eyes.

Nolan continued. "You said someone named Wu can tell me what I need to know about the wormholes out there. I want to meet with him."

"He's in Moon City, but I should tell you that he hasn't been himself since the accident. He's…scrambled."

"I'll deal with that when it comes up. Right now, we need to get to the Moon. What are our options?"

Edward smiled, and laughed a little. "We need Elena on this."

30

Nora looked out over the refugee camp from her suite inside the QuestCorp compound. A bowl of apples rested on a small table nearby. A look of sorrow covered her face. The camp was an abomination of civilization visible only by the light of small fires glowing below the tented peaks of the camp quarters. The camp stretched out into the darkness, and the glow from the fires shone as small specks well into the distance. Without a way to move any of these people, the camp would be their forever home. She looked up. The sky above the camp was empty. It was black. No stars, or Moon, or light of any kind shone down on the dark world below. There was a knock at the door. Eli entered.

"Hello, Nora."

Nora didn't answer or turn from the window.

Eli cleared his throat, annoyed. "How's the view? You've got the best suite in the facility."

She still didn't turn. "Like a princess locked away in a tower."

Eli snorted a laugh. He walked over to the apples, picked one up and took a huge bite. "These are so good. Better than anything I ever had on Earth. Moon City farmers really know what they are doing. I think even my father would be impressed."

"What do you want, Eli?"

"I'm just here to thank you. Luring Nolan off the wall and starting that riot gave me valuable insight into the people's mindset. They rose up quickly against S.W.A.R.M. when they saw him in trouble. At some point, we will have to turn them all against him. Offering him the apple was a nice touch."

Nora turned to look at Eli, now sitting in a chair facing her. "They love him. They think *he* is going to save them. Not you."

"It doesn't matter. Let them think that. It will keep them subdued. We need the time anyway. Chance won't budge on the wormhole cache. He's keeping it locked. We need to go there and break in. I need you to make sure the job gets done."

Nora's eyes and brow locked as she stared at Eli with unadulterated hate. "Send your damn robots. I'm not going."

Eli smiled and laughed. "Don't do it for me, do it for yourself. Rid yourself of the heartache you feel for all those people out there living in tents."

"No."

"No?" Eli feigned surprise.

"No. I am not helping you anymore."

Eli levied an evil grin in the face of her defiance. "I can, and will, make you do this. You said you wouldn't help me lure Nolan off the wall and look how much you invested in that little performance. If you think I was hard on you before, you haven't seen the worst. You are going to Venus with the team. You will oversee their operation and transmit to me daily. I want to know everything that is being done. Despite your lack of enthusiasm for my plan, I know you can at least handle that. And, you'll be somewhere I won't have to constantly find you."

"I AM NOT HELPING YOU!" Nora screamed, grabbing the bowl of apples and hurling it at Eli. He held up his forearm.

Angered, he stood up, leaned into Nora and grabbed her by the collar, pulling her close so that they stood eye to eye. "I will personally place you on the flight to Venus, binding you to a chair with instructions that you not be untied until arrival. You don't have a say in this. I call the shots. You do the work. *That* will never change."

Nora spit in Eli's face, and pushed him off her. Eli regained his composure, but grimaced as he wiped his face clean with his hand, all the while staring at her. Nora didn't flinch.

"You're on the next flight to the Moon," Eli said, "and from there it's Venus." He walked out of the room, sending in S.W.A.R.M. as he left.

31

Sylas was in line, hobbling his way into the refugee camp behind a wheelchair filled with blankets and food. The procession of people entering the camp in front and behind him was endless. As he passed the gates that lead into the QuestCorp facility, S.W.A.R.M. robots armed with machine guns stood on the wall that separated the facility and the camp. It was a slow walk, as the volume of people moving through made anything but a snail's pace impossible. The pace suited him, though. The bloodstains on his pants surrounded a hole that looked like it came from a blunt puncture wound. The wheelchair did a good job supporting his weight as he pushed it along.

The people around him weren't much better off. They were weary and afraid. Sylas kept his focus elsewhere, trying to ignore them. Along the corridor that lead into the camp, televisions broadcasted welcome messages to the arrivals, repeating the same series of images over and over, each time accompanied by a different language. Images of family dinners and sunlit meadows wove together with video of QuestCorp hydrogen deliveries and S.W.A.R.M. relief efforts. Sylas watched, but didn't understand the Asian languages cycling through. The queue made a sharp turn away from the wall, into the rows of tents. The televisions no longer lined the path.

As he moved deeper into the camp S.W.A.R.M. robots surveilled closely. People sat in and around each tent, and a small fire burning outside the openings kept people warm. Sylas heard them talking quietly among their groups, and only among their groups. They despondently watched him and the others in the procession. There was no compassion or anger in their stares, just apathy. The queue kept moving, trudging its way to the outer ring of the refugee camp.

At the edge of the camp were empty tents, as well as more tents being raised by countless S.W.A.R.M. robots. The queue split in two, S.W.A.R.M. directing half along one leg of the outer tent ring, and half along the other. Sylas watched as families were assigned to tents one by one as the line stretched into the empty row. As it thinned he came closer to the front, yet was held to the side so families could be kept together. As sporadic lone travelers emerged from the queue they were pulled out and placed beside Sylas. Once there were four standing together, a S.W.A.R.M. bot addressed them.

"You will be assigned to quarters together. Please return to the line and stay together."

The robot applied a bright orange sticker that had the number H-894 and a barcode on it to each of their chests, then motioned for them to move along. Sylas and his new tent mates reentered the line and continued moving down the row. He looked up and watched a low-flying shuttle pass by and land inside the QuestCorp walls.

32

Everything seemed timeless in the world of night. Nolan tried to note the passing of time by tracking the shuttle flights from Moon City as he heard them pass over the lab. Nolan's fruitless effort to understand his father's forgotten language within the alien computer had become a mind-numbing waste of his ambition. His future was clear. He wasn't going to end his days working in a research lab for Eli. He would end his days opening the door for everyone else's future. He never chose Earth as his home, but he felt indebted to the world that taught him his humanity.

The hours Nolan and Edward spent reviewing the crystal's scientific data had been peppered with casual conversation. Over a working dinner, Edward had told Nolan about his wife.

"You'll love Elena," he said. "She's fearless. Prudent, but fearless. Very take charge. When we originally came here, we weren't allowed to see each other. Those were truly dark days."

Nolan kept his eyes on his work. "I can imagine."

Edward huffed a laugh. "I can't believe I haven't asked before, but do you have someone, Nolan?"

"No. No wife or anything like that. Just my mother, Mariel."

"Do you know if she's okay?"

"No." Nolan continued to focus on the data he was viewing.

"Well, have hope. Sorry to ask."

Nolan turned to Edward. "How is Elena? Were you reunited?"

Edward smiled, then looked down sheepishly. "Yes. Thankfully. Eli had us separated and interrogated, but eventually he put us back together."

"That seems uncharacteristic of Eli."

"I suppose, but credit where credit is due. I think he knew our work would be better if he kept us together. We are a great team."

"I'm sure he recognized that. I'm happy you have each other."

"Thank you. She's a bit of sunshine in this otherwise dreary world, I suppose."

A pause came over the conversation as they went back to their work. Suddenly, Edward slid his chair over to Nolan and began talking quietly so that the S.W.A.R.M. bots monitoring them would have difficulty recording the conversation.

"Elena has mapped out a plan to seize the lunar shuttle, and to get to the ICS using Helios, the solar sailing ship docked at Moon City." Edward glanced at S.W.A.R.M. again, and then looked intently at Nolan, and whispered, "You are the key to the plan's success." Looking square into Nolan's eyes, Edward nodded with a near maniacal smile as he rolled his chair back to his workstation.

Leaning back toward Edward, Nolan began picking at the details, skeptical of Edward's understanding of the task he was asking Nolan to undertake.

"What do you do when the shuttle lands? How do you get on board? How do you fly away? What do you do once you've reached the Moon? Do you think S.W.A.R.M. is just going to sit in standby mode? And you know they can hear us whispering right now, right?"

Edward glanced at the robots again, and then looked back at Nolan. "It doesn't matter. We have you. We'll fight our way on. All of us. S.W.A.R.M. certainly isn't going to let us just walk on, I know that, but this place has made you strong again. And once you get to the Moon you will be out from under the cloud permanently.

Rejuvenated. The game changes in our favor at that point."

"What about you and Elena?"

"She'll keep us safe. We'll be behind you all the way. Once we are off Earth I will find the solution that will fix the sky."

Nolan shook his head, irritated by Edward's insistence on undoing the damage brought on by the cloud. "Moon City must have security," He said, changing the subject.

Edward nodded. "Like you've never seen. You'll be fine though."

Nolan looked at Edward contemplatively, unsure of him, as if he was sizing him up. Edward sat up straight. "I'm not afraid, Nolan. I want to do this," he said, his eyes welling up. "My science did this. The darkness, the wormhole troubles, everything. I never set out to destroy anything."

"Yet here we are."

"Precisely! Here we are; you and me. We may have started out on opposite sides of this conflict, but we have a common enemy, and a common goal. There is something to be said about that. It's like, fate or something."

"It's called maximum security, Edward. Eli has placed all of his assets where he can easily monitor them."

Edward was getting frustrated. "We've got to do this, Nolan. It's meant to be."

Nolan looked down at the crystal set on his workstation. "This crystal has shown me a part of my life I'd never known before. It all feels pretty removed from the life I've lived here on Earth, but seeing what happened to Oua makes me want to save everyone I can even more."

Edward smiled at Nolan's warm thoughts. "You have a lot of hope."

"It's not hope, Edward. It's perspective."

"Well, I have hope. I believe we *can* fix things. We can get it done together. It's not like we have a nuclear bomb to deal with. It's just a little cloud, right?"

Nolan didn't laugh at Edward's callous assessment. Edward quickly got serious as he reviewed the challenges he faced with Nolan. "Without Arthur, I don't know how to open the wormhole cache once we reach Venus."

"Where is Arthur?"

"I don't know."

"Can you bypass?"

"Yes and no." Edward cringed as he spoke to Nolan. His plan stopped short, as if it faced a wall that stretched out each way without revealing which way was shortest, or best.

Nolan wasn't fazed by the uncertainty. "There's no bargaining with Eli," he said, "but clearly he doesn't want any of us dead. I'm guessing your friend Arthur wouldn't help him, otherwise you might just be another refugee in the camp right now. It seems to me, in any scenario, you are going to wind up at the wormhole control station. Either with me or with Eli. Either way, it's a shot at saving mankind." Edward took a moment, and Nolan reiterated his point. "It's a chance to save lives."

Edward's eyes looked about wildly as Nolan drove his points home. "Right. If the wormhole is restored and Eli brings everyone to the new world, yes, everything will be okay in that regard. But, if I am successful then Earth lives, and so do you."

"Don't worry about me."

"Well, I am worried. I've seen a lot of the universe working for QuestCorp. I've lost some people along the way. It's not something I want to deal with again."

"Focus on what you need to do. Once I'm away from the cloud you won't have to worry about me."

A look of guilt came over Edward's face. "Nolan, my team and I altered the Elijum molecularly, making it unstable. When it was released into the atmosphere, it sought to stabilize itself, so it bonded with decaying ozone molecules. We designed the molecular bond to be irreversible, but I have a theory of how I might reverse it. The material we used to make the cloud was found in a debris field left from when Oua was destroyed. Whatever caused the heavy concentration of Elijum there might also work to repel it if manipulated correctly. I'll have to run tests. After I find what I am looking for."

Nolan snapped at Edward. "You are reckless and unfocused."

"I'm doing my best," Edward said, snapping back immediately.

"You don't see your own flaws. You want to save the world on a hunch."

"I know my flaws. I know when I am wrong. I wouldn't put a world of people in jeopardy to test a theory."

"I'm sorry, Edward, but catastrophe has surrounded your work. You are more interested in the theory than its effects."

Edward stood, no longer focused on being quiet. "Catastrophes happen when the work is *rushed*. I did what I was supposed to do." Edward stormed toward the exit, but was stopped by S.W.A.R.M. "Let me out, you recycled motorcycle!" He shouted, throwing papers from a nearby desk at the robots.

Nolan didn't try to intervene as Edward was grabbed and escorted from the lab. The remaining bot focused on him, aiming an ion gun at him. Nolan sat, placing his hands in the air slightly as he did. The robot backed down and resumed its post.

Nolan went back to the data he was viewing before his conversation with Edward. It was a video of his father demonstrating the gravitational pulls of the sun and the gas giant that eventually pulled his world apart. He paused the video on an image of his father, then let out a sigh. "This whole thing is crazy."

A voice chimed in from behind him. "It's revolutionary." Eli was standing in the doorway, leaning against the jamb. "I'm sure you realize I hear everything. I don't know why you let Edward go on for so long."

Nolan gave Eli a glare, and then turned back at his workstation. "He had something to say. It was worth hearing."

"Was it?" Eli entered the room and stood next to Nolan.

Nolan turned. "This camp is not much of a life by any means. From my post, I saw the faces of the refugees when they passed. They were crushed, and hopeless. Most never even bothered to look at me as they walked by. Before you blotted out the Sun, people embraced me without truly understanding what I was or how I could do what no other man could do. And I did all I could to live up to that. Under this cloud though, I'm nothing but another refugee wishing for brighter days, and trying to stay alive. I want to be the man who helps them all, but you have a better shot at saving mankind than I do. I want to help you get everyone off Earth."

Eli laughed, boastfully. "I don't need your help, alien."

"You do. You need my help with the wormhole cache. I know about the fourth dimension, and the trouble it caused."

Eli's joviality quickly subdued. Nolan continued. "You need the wormholes. I will get them back, so you can save mankind."

Eli had no reply, but the look on his face conveyed controlled anger. "What makes you think you can do anything to help?"

"I know that you can't do anything, otherwise you'd have done it by now. And, I don't know if I can either, which is why you should send Edward and Elena with me. If I fail, then Edward can start up a new wormhole."

"They want to save Earth. I'm not interested in that."

"I don't think there is anything left on Earth worth saving other than the people on it. I'll see to it that they are on the same page, whatever it takes."

Eli paused. "There is no way I would ever let you steal my shuttle. I am intrigued, however, as to how well you can perform against our problem in the fourth dimension. You just might be of use yet, alien."

33

Nolan had done his best all his life to learn as many languages as he could, but was still surprised by how many languages were spoken among all the refugees in the camp. Body language filled the gaps for what he couldn't understand. He was happy to be out and meeting people while helping S.W.A.R.M. with meal service, but was eager to finish up and then meet with Edward and Elena to discuss the plan to get to Venus. The volume of refugees in the camp was increasing endlessly. He had spent his adulthood saving people from the worst fates imaginable but had never saved a planet's worth of lives. He met Edward and Elena for dinner in the dining tent when service was nearly over.

"Nolan, allow me to introduce my wife, Elena," Edward said as Nolan joined them at a table.

Nolan extended his hand. "Hello. It's nice to meet you. Edward has told me a lot about you."

Smiling, Elena shook his hand. "Thank you. Nice to meet you too." She looked around, noting that S.W.A.R.M. was nearby, but not too close. She leaned into Nolan, and whispered, "Edward tells me you and he have a plan to save Earth?"

Nolan was caught off guard, but not surprised that Edward framed the plan as being Nolan's. Nonetheless, he laid it all out. "I'll help you get to Venus, but the mission is the people, not the planet. Let's make that clear."

"Oh, come on!" Edward said.

"Why not?" Elena followed.

"The atmosphere is poison now, not just for me, but for everyone. Radiation will eventually catch up to all of us. My only priority is helping Eli get the people off Earth.

The scientists momentarily sat in a silent mixture of disbelief and defiance. Edward shook his head and tried to explain his position to Nolan again. "No, no. It's simple, Nolan. We must use the cache to find the answers we need. If there is anything that can undo what has been done, it is out there. You have to help us access the cache so that we can begin searching for a solution."

"We'll go to the cache. I will fight whatever is in there; whatever got your friend Wu, but then we open the wormhole to the new world. There is no fight for Earth."

Elena spoke up. "I found the planet for Eli; the new one he wants to take everyone to. I have been there and have seen where mankind is headed. It is a glorious world, but this is mankind's home." Elena pointed to the ground.

Nolan pointed to the sky. "You made this cloud to kill the planet, and in that you've succeeded. But there is no reason for the people to suffer from it. This whole event is bigger than either of you, or me. You need to know where you can make a difference and where you've been beaten."

"Give science the chance to fix things," Edward said.

"You're not using science here. You're going on hope," Nolan fired back.

Edward stood up abruptly, his legs pushing the chair backward. "It's theory! Together, maybe we could've have fixed things, but you won't even try! What kind of a hero are you? The cloud is here because of both of us. We should be fighting it!"

"Edward, calm down. You're getting loud," Elena said.

Edward looked toward the S.W.A.R.M. bots serving the refugees. One turned his way, so he sat back down. It resumed its service.

Nolan was frustrated by the conversation. "What about Wu? Edward, you said I should meet him. If Wu can help, we need to know. Let's get to him in Moon City.

Once we hear what he has to say, we can decide from there what we do when we reach the cache."

Elena looked uncertain. "You have no idea what the fight even is in front of you," she said to Nolan.

Nolan was steadfast. "It's a fight for life. That's all I need to know. This isn't a debate," he said. "We are going to Moon City to find Wu. I'll let you know when the time is right." Nolan stood. "If you'll excuse me."

He walked away, leaving the two scientists staring at one another, stewing.

34

Eli called a meeting with Nolan and Nora to discuss the mission to Venus, meeting them together in a conference room. S.W.A.R.M. lined the wall behind him. The plan to fulfill his vision was once again showing promise, but there were still loose ends. A wormhole to transport the world's population was within reach, provided Nolan could neutralize whatever was lurking in the fourth dimension near the cache. Still, Eli wanted Nora to oversee the mission.

"I wanted the two of you to meet," he said. "My former right hand and my former enemy, nearly reversed in position." Nolan and Nora, sitting across the table from Eli, looked at one another and nodded. Eli continued.

"Nora, Nolan is going with you, Edward, and Elena to the ICS. He is going to get rid of our problem within the fourth dimension. I want you to bring Wu as well. He might be useful. The moment Nolan clears out the problem I want Edward and Wu to activate the wormhole to the new world. I want it opened here at this facility. Here are the coordinates." Eli handed Nora a note with numbers written on it. He then turned and looked at Nolan. "Wu is the key. Give him my best when you get to Moon City." Eli paused for a moment, looking at Nolan with doubt. "Can you do this?"

Nolan looked at Eli with sharp eyes, answering him squarely. "If I can't, then it can't be done."

Eli wasn't amused. "This changes nothing. You won't earn a ride to the new world by doing this."

"I'm not doing it for that. I'm doing it because it's what needs to be done."

Eli smirked at Nolan, but then his face grew long. "As long as we're clear."

Nora couldn't stay quiet any longer. "He is your only chance at fixing this, Eli, and you won't even let him come along? I refuse to do *anything* to help you."

Eli responded firmly. "Fail to perform and I will leave you behind. You will be the last of mankind in this solar system."

Nora shook her head in disgust. "Everyone is doomed from the start, even if they help you. And without Arthur, you can't even get in. Where is Arthur?"

Eli rolled his tongue inside his mouth and gave Nora a cold stare. "Unavailable."

Eli read Nora's disapproval, and changed the subject. He turned to Nolan. "I know you've already made things clear to him, but lay off Edward. Let him have his hope. I need his head to be on straight at the ICS."

"I'll handle Edward," Nolan said. "I'm not worried."

Eli's doubt showed on his face. "I'll arrange a flight, but I don't want Edward and Elena to know I have sanctioned this trip. They are motivated by their rebelliousness. Keep that going. Make it feel … authentic."

Nolan looked at Eli starkly. "I want your word that my mother will make the trip."

"I will have S.W.A.R.M. collect her and bring her to the camp." Eli waited for a reaction from Nolan, but none came. "Once she is here, our alliance is over." Eli got up from the table, and on his way out of the conference room briefly addressed Nolan again. "Be careful, alien. I'd hate to lose an employee on the job," he said, and then left.

35

Nolan met Edward and Elena at the main gate of the QuestCorp facility after finishing up another food service. He didn't waste any time once he saw them. "It's time. The shuttle came in this morning and is preparing for the return flight now."

"We need guns," Elena said, assertively. She caught Nolan off guard, and he hesitated to respond. Noting his reaction, Elena continued in more detail. "We need firearms. The S.W.A.R.M. armory isn't far. How fast can you make it there and back?"

Nolan's eyes widened, and he quickly tried to simmer Elena's energy. "I don't think we'll need guns, Elena. I can teleport with each of you under one arm. We can be on the shuttle before S.W.A.R.M. even realizes what's happening."

Elena shook her head in disagreement. "Edward has a pacemaker. He can't take the jolt. Let's get moving. If S.W.A.R.M. is on high alert, we may have already tipped it off by talking right now. And, who's to say we won't need guns once we are on the shuttle? Or the Moon? S.W.A.R.M. could be anywhere."

"Okay," Nolan said. "I see your point."

Nolan knew the location of the armory. It was in the middle of the QuestCorp compound, a short run from where they now stood. He made the jolt to the armory in one jump. It was the longest jump he'd made in a while, and despite being part of a ruse to fool the scientists, it made him feel good, as though he was normal again.

When he reached the armory, he found two S.W.A.R.M. robots guarding the entrance. He grabbed them as soon as he materialized next to them, and instantly teleported with them high into the sky, letting them go before disappearing once again in a field of raw electricity. He was down on the ground with weapons in hand before they even crashed back to Earth. Once the bots were offline, however, a technical alarm registered which notified S.W.A.R.M. entirely. Nolan held a couple of M-16s along with some ammunition. He'd never transported any kind of explosive by teleportation before and wasn't sure if the ammo would be damaged or discharged by the massive electrical charge he generated when he jumped, so he decided to run it all back. Along the way, he briefly thought about how Edward and Elena were scientists, and not prepared for the very real chance of a fight with S.W.A.R.M. Elena had a somewhat level head, but Edward was a wildcard. He hoped that Edward wouldn't hurt himself, or anyone else, once he had a gun in hand.

The doctors were waiting for him when he ran up to the gates of the QuestCorp complex on the edge of the refugee camp. As he reached them he handed over the rifles, as well as a nine-millimeter to Elena. Elena checked the magazine, cocked the gun, and disengaged the safety immediately. She did the same for Edward. "Let's go," she said, and then turned to run toward the shuttle. Edward stayed on her hip, and Nolan quickly found himself moving to get ahead of them. Even after he got out in front, the doctors followed his footsteps so closely that a single misstep might put them in his boots. He looked back at them and noticed Edward had a look of sheer panic and terror on his face, clearly not knowing what to expect during the sprint to the shuttle. Elena kept him moving forward at a fast pace, though. When the team was just a few yards from the launch pad, the alarms ceased and S.W.A.R.M. began pouring out from every door nearby, surrounding the ship's landing platform like a flood.

Elena fired her rifle immediately. The S.W.A.R.M. robots were fast and technologically advanced, but not very well protected from the spray of bullets, so after a few penetrating rounds they dropped to the ground in fits of malfunction. Reinforcements arrived as quickly as they were dropped, moving in on Nolan and the scientists as a uniform cluster of metal and wire. Nolan saw the bulky herd of automated brawlers fixed on him and yelled to the others to make a run for the shuttle. He dug his feet into the ground and readied himself to take on the robot horde. S.W.A.R.M. crashed down on him like a giant wave, and as cold metal hands began grasping, tearing, and punching, Nolan tore in, ripping away chunks of robot piece by piece. More robots entered the fight as he continued to tear at them as though he himself was a machine performing some routine, repetitive task. Registering the stalemate, S.W.A.R.M. redirected its attention to the scientists nearing the shuttle.

A robot grabbed Edward by the back of his shirt and tossed him through the air back toward the rumble. Nolan saw this, and broke away from the fight, quickly jolting to Edward with a quick teleport and cradling him in his arms before he hit the ground. Elena took out the squadron surrounding her, and then, after picking up the rifle Edward had dropped, targeted the wave of robots headed toward Nolan and her husband, spraying dual cover fire as she ran back toward them, reloading along the way. When she reached them, she grabbed Edward from Nolan and lead him away. "Get on the shuttle," Nolan shouted before grabbing the two M-16's from her and blasting S.W.A.R.M. with rapid fire. Elena ran Edward out under the cover fire as Nolan emptied the gun's magazines into the robot horde. He created a large enough gap for the two to get away before S.W.A.R.M. advanced and covered him in a mound of metal and mayhem once again.

Nolan jolted out from underneath them, but as quickly as he teleported nearer the ship S.W.A.R.M. reformed a mound on top of him. S.W.A.R.M. tried to send some robots into the shuttle to stop flight preparations, but Nolan burst through the pile, grabbed the wayward robots, and disposed of them in a permanent fashion, hurling the short-circuited hunks of metal back at the horde. A big smile came across his face. He felt his strength in every punch and throw, and though he wasn't back to his fittest, he felt like himself again. However, since he didn't know if he'd be successful destroying whatever was in the wormhole cache when he got to Venus, he didn't want to destroy too much of the S.W.A.R.M. force.

The engines of the shuttle roared to life, and after landing one last, solid punch, he grabbed the nearest robot, swung it up and around his head several times and then released it into the wave of robots barreling down on him, knocking down the entire frontline. It gave him just enough time to jolt into the shuttle and slam the door shut. As soon as he was on board, he shouted to the flight commander to fire the thrusters. Edward and Elena were strapped into chairs behind him. Elena held her pistol firmly pointed at the back of the commander's head, a look of panic and remorse on her face. As the shuttle began its liftoff, S.W.A.R.M. jumped and grabbed at it, but the blast from the engines either blew the robots back or burned them up. Nolan moved toward Elena and took the handgun from her. He then checked on Edward, finding him strapped into a seat, seemingly unharmed, but scared out of his mind.

Nolan looked at the shuttle commander and laughed out loud. "Hello, Armstrong."

Armstrong was focused on the takeoff. "Nolan," he answered.

Edward looked at Elena, somewhat confused.

"You know him?" Elena asked Nolan.

Nolan smiled, and sat back in a seat. "We are in good hands."

The ship rocketed off the planet, and when it cleared the atmosphere, Armstrong shouted back to Nolan. "Where to?"

"To the Moon, and into some sunshine," he said with a smile.

36

Nora wasn't going to Venus; there was no way she was taking part in Eli's vision anymore. He destroyed the world she loved, and she didn't want to bear witness to anything else he was capable of doing. From her quarters, she looked out at the shuttle being prepped for its return flight to Moon City. A small, packed bag rested on her bed.

S.W.A.R.M. was posted outside her door. She had no access to resources within the facility but could come and go to a certain extent, always followed by her robot watchdogs. Ditching S.W.A.R.M. again would be near impossible, but it was worth a shot. She just needed a distraction.

Before Eli could give S.W.A.R.M. the command to collect her and place her on the shuttle, she grabbed her bag and left her room. Alarms were sounding, but they rang in the background of her determination to escape. Two S.W.A.R.M. bots followed her as she walked calmly down the corridor, acting as though all was normal, though small beads of sweat began to form on her forehead. The stairwell at the end of the hall took her outside to a small courtyard in the center of the QuestCorp complex. As she crossed the complex, she could see the top of the shuttle rising above the other buildings in the facility. She was making her way toward it when she heard gunfire. Flinching at the sound of the fighting, she instinctually crouched down and halted. She'd heard attacks like this before, but she'd always been a safe distance away, or at least able to run. Realizing the opportunity for a distraction, she stood and continued to walk toward the shuttle, the sounds of the battle growing louder.

As she neared the edge of the courtyard she entered a breezeway that led to the shuttle landing pad. It was there that she finally saw the commotion; it wasn't another siege attempt from the refugee camp. Nolan was fighting his way through S.W.A.R.M. The two bots following her didn't react to the fighting, however she did hear Eli's voice through their speakers.

"Hold her."

The two robots grabbed her by the arms. She struggled to pull away, but it was a lost cause. She looked around, and saw Eli slowly approach from a darkened corner nearby. As he approached, he noticed her packed bag. "You packed for Venus," he said smugly. He looked over at the battle underway, then back at Nora. "Looks like you're running late. This heist is certainly … authentic."

"I don't want any part of what you are doing. Savior probably doesn't either."

Eli smiled. "Actually, he's very much on board with my plan, though he did start a fight with S.W.A.R.M. He's just doing things his way, it seems." He paced slowly in front of her, hands behind his back. "I knew you'd run again." He looked at the S.W.A.R.M. bots holding her. "Load her on the shuttle. Don't let her get hurt in the fray." He looked back at Nora. "Act like you snuck on like the rest of them once you are onboard."

As he spoke, a stream of gunfire rattled off from the fight. A command came across the intercom on the S.W.A.R.M. bots that held her: *"Reinforcements required."* The robots faced Eli. He waved them on. "Go," he said, then looking at Nora; "I'll make sure she makes the flight." They released Nora and headed toward the battle. Nora began rubbing her arm where she had been held. She looked at Eli with disdain.

"Even if you get me on that shuttle you can't make me help you," she said through gritted teeth.

"I can do anything," Eli said, pulling a handgun from behind, and aiming it at her. "And you will do whatever I say, or you will spend the rest of your days confined to a room with no view, with nothing but a mining drone for company." He paused and smiled at her, then ran the gun's muzzle along her cheek. "I know how much you miss all the pretty things from this world. I'd hate to see you miss out on all of them on the next one too."

Nora let out a warrior's scream and grabbed Eli's hand that held the gun. She twisted his arm around behind his back, loosening his grip on the gun so she could grab it. She pressed it against his temple as she pulled him down and in, close to her body. Eli struggled and broke loose, though. As he turned to face her, she smashed him in the face with the grip. He fell to the ground.

Nora ran into the shuttle launch area, but S.W.A.R.M. paid no attention to her. It was fully engaged with Nolan. She ran along the wall of a building toward the QuestCorp gates that emptied into the refugee camp, keeping as far away from the fighting as she could. As she ran, she heard Eli yell from somewhere behind her. She looked back and saw a handful of S.W.A.R.M. bots break off from the mound and move toward her. She ran through the gates and into the camp before they could get close.

A heavy crowd of people were gathered near the gate, alerted to the fighting happening inside. Nora moved through them swiftly. S.W.A.R.M. rammed its way through the crowd, mercilessly tossing people out of its way, but the volume of people slowed it down nonetheless. Nora put some distance between her and the robot squadron, but it wasn't long before a handful more jumped down into the camp from the complex wall to join the pursuit, landing directly behind her as she ran. She dodged one attempt at a grab, then ran off the main camp avenue into the rings of tent rows, which encircled the QuestCorp facility. Nora ran through row after row, randomly turning corners and passing in and out of the tents as she tried to outrun the robots. S.W.A.R.M stayed close, continuing to push through crowds and tear through tents. They could easily track her, but she had the advantage of being smaller and more agile. Once there was a good distance between her and them, she decided to hide in one of the tents. She randomly picked one and jumped in, and as she crouched down on her knees alongside a makeshift bed, she motioned to the family that occupied the tent to be quiet. They looked terrified. Everyone in the tent could hear the nearby refugees being thrown aside and families being cast from their tents. Nora stared at the family, noticing how the children were just as frightened as she was. Nora mouthed 'I'm sorry' to the mother, but she just stared back, petrified.

Nora stood to exit the tent when the father of the family spoke. "Stoppe," he said. Nora recognized the accent as Nordic. "Vente," he said, putting his hand out, his palm facing her. The man then stood up. He looked over at his family, who was crouched in the corner of the tent. "Jeg elsker deg," he said, and then exited the tent. Once outside he began shouting. Nora looked through the tent flap and saw him running toward the S.W.A.R.M. force, picking up a wooden log as he charged, raising it high above his head. S.W.A.R.M. reacted, grabbing him by the neck and wrist before he could strike. Men and women surrounding the scene immediately began to attack the robots in an attempt to free the man. Nora looked back at the man's family and motioned for them to follow her. Together they ran from the tent and toward the border of the refugee camp. Gunshots rang out almost immediately from the area they had just left. The mother screamed out, fearing for her husband. They continued to run until they disappeared into the darkness, gone before S.W.A.R.M. could even pursue them.

37

Eli entered the small office where Arthur was being held and sat down across the table from him. Thanks to Nora, he had a black eye, and looked madder than usual. Initially he only glared at Arthur, who in turn glared back. "You depleted my tolerance long ago, Arthur. Tell me how to access the cache, and you will see the other side of this."

Arthur, weak and doubled over from exhaustion and dehydration, nested his head in his arms as he folded them on the desk.

"Go to hell," he said, faintly, speaking into the desk.

A growl came from Eli as he exhaled. The standoff between them was locked in its course. He stood, and walked over to sit next to a sleep deprived and starved Arthur. He leaned in close and spoke softly. "I am going to explain this to you. All you have to do is listen. After you've heard what I have to say, if you want to tell me anything, I will be happy to hear it." He then spoke sternly. "The future will be of *my* design, Arthur. No roadblock along the way will stop me from getting there. You feel valiant; like you are doing something good. Something right. But you are wrong. This world is over. Even Savior, your great hero, agrees with me. He is on his way to Venus right now with Edward and Elena to clear the cache. You can't undo this destruction. Everything here will eventually die, but you can save what is left by helping them. You can give us the wormhole we need and then *you* will be a hero. Then everyone lives. Even you. And I will be fair with you once we are there. All your poor decisions can be wiped away in one single act of good. Unlock the cache. Send us all home."

Arthur didn't move but started to breathe heavily. On the desk, his hands balled into fists. Eli placed his hand on the back of Arthur's head. "You are making this decision. Not me. Thank you for everything you've done to help me. Your hard work will be remembered." Eli stood up from the table and exited the room. As he left, he spoke to S.W.A.R.M., standing guard outside the meeting room.

"Shoot him."

"Command cannot be completed. Command requires system override of safety protocol."

Eli let out a primordial scream at the robot and snatched the rifle it was holding. He aimed it at the robot and without hesitation emptied a magazine into it. It dropped to the ground like a puppet with no strings. Eli walked over to it and grabbed another magazine attached to its torso and reloaded the gun. He reentered the meeting room, stood behind Arthur, and aimed the gun.

"A new world awaits. You can't stop a Quest," he said, and then fired.

38

Nora ran for hours before she stopped. In the never-ending night it was impossible to tell just how long and how far she'd gone, but stopping was not an option. S.W.A.R.M. never followed her out of the refugee camp, but it had a talent for finding her. For this reason, any rest she took was short lived, even though the family she fled with struggled to keep pace.

Stopping for a rest at the edge of a dead cornfield bordering an old forest, Nora took a moment to size up who was dragging along with her to escape; it was the least she could do to honor the father's sacrifice. The mother sat on the ground holding her children in her lap, both speaking to her through tears. She consoled them, holding their heads and rocking them back and forth. Neither of them looked older than eight or nine. She watched as the Nordic family huddled together and consoled one another, but knew she had more pressing problems to solve like how to keep everyone alive on a dead planet.

As the reality of the moment set in, Nora began to tear up. She turned away from the family so they couldn't see her cry, and did her best to compose herself as quickly as possible. The more she fought back the harder she cried, though. She soon found herself sobbing, overcome with the emotions she'd held on to ever since Eli revealed his plan to release the cloud. She was suddenly startled by the mother's hand on her shoulder. She turned and saw the entire family standing at her side.

"I'm sorry," she said. "I'm okay. I'm okay."

Tears continued to stream from her eyes, anguish covering her face. The mother embraced her, giving her a long, heartfelt hug. The children leaned in and followed.

"Silje," the woman said, pulling away from Nora and touching her chest as she spoke. "Silje."

Nora followed suit and introduced herself to the family in the same manner. The children smiled when she did, and each took turns introducing themselves as well.

"Laila," the little girl said, half hiding behind her mother's leg.

"Hello, Laila," Nora said, crouching down to eye level with her.

"Rolf!" Said her brother, tapping excitedly on his chest, then added some words in English. "I am boy!" He shouted, blurting out the words in an awkward manner.

It was hard not to laugh, and once Nora did, the family joined in; a moment of levity in the face of all the intensity of their current circumstance.

"We need to find food," Nora said, motioning with her fingers toward her mouth. "Food."

"Mat," the woman replied, mimicking Nora's gesture.

Nora nodded, and then motioned for the family to follow her as she began to walk along the edge of the field. Nothing was alive. The corn in the field, along with the trees in the adjacent forest, had all died under the cloud. Their best hope was finding a farmstead and searching the buildings.

Nora lead the family, and it wasn't long before they came to a farmhouse. The door was open, but all the lights were off. There was no power. A house this close to the refugee camp was sure to be uninhabited, having already been searched by S.W.A.R.M. for occupants to transport to the camp, and its power pulled once it was cleared. Yet, the house also posed a danger, because S.W.A.R.M. would be looking for Nora, likely surveilling houses like this in the area. A good distance from the house, she gathered the family, and had everyone crouch in the cornfield. She cautioned them to be quiet, and then watched the house. There was no activity. She didn't hear any heavy metal footfalls, nor did she hear any comm chatter. If S.W.A.R.M. was inside, they were programmed to ambush. Nora looked toward the family, which was staring at her.

"Go," she said, pointing to the house. "Go. Food. Mat."

They all just kept staring.

"Please," she continued, "go in the house. Mat. Mat," she said, repeatedly moving her closed hand toward her mouth.

Silje pointed at Nora and then pointed at the house, signaling she wanted everyone to go together. Nora shook her head, and then pointed to herself and then at the ground where they were. Then she pointed at the two kids and said, "Mat," before pointing at the house again. Silje looked unsure. Nora pointed two fingers to her eyes, and then out into the darkness, signaling to Silje that she would be a lookout for the family as they looked for food inside the house. Silje nodded to show that she now understood and began to usher her children toward the farmhouse. Nora watched them as they made their way.

The family reached the opened door and walked into the house. Instantly, spotlights turned on from within and a tin voice began speaking.

"You are not in danger. Please accompany us to the QuestCorp facility for food and shelter."

Silje and the children screamed, frightened by the sudden appearance of the S.W.A.R.M. bots that had been in standby mode in the house, just as Nora had suspected. The robots began to move toward the family and Rolf decided to run. He sprinted into the cornfield and crouched down as his mother yelled to him. One S.W.A.R.M. bot grabbed Silje and her daughter by the arms, and the others moved into the field to pursue the boy. Nora saw this and panicked. She had to get away or risk recapture, but didn't want to give her position up to S.W.A.R.M. She laid down on her belly to obscure her even more from sight. Silje was at the house screaming for her son while her daughter was fearfully crying in S.W.A.R.M.'s clutches.

The S.W.A.R.M. bots in the field were moving slowly through the rows of dead corn, shining their lights from side to side. Rolf was hidden well, but the cornfield was small. Nora was out of danger for the moment since S.W.A.R.M. was moving in the opposite direction, so she decided to slide backward to get to the far corner of the field where she would have the shortest distance to cover on foot to the old dead forest. Slowly, she pushed herself back with her hands, trying to not make a sound. Silje and Laila's cries helped dampen the sound of the cracking sticks and the rustling dead weeds.

She was near the corner of the field when she heard something moving closer to her from a few rows over. She stopped moving, not knowing what was approaching. Luckily, S.W.A.R.M.'s lights were still shining away from her on the other side of the field. As she laid still the rustling grew louder. She started to hear a frantic breathing pattern. She turned herself around to face the corner of the cornfield where she had planned to make her exit, and then got up into a crouched position. As she was getting ready to make a sprint, Rolf emerged, which startled them both. He panicked, but Nora placed her hand over his mouth. But it was too late. The heavy footfalls of S.W.A.R.M. were moving toward them. She grabbed his wrist, stood him up, and got him running toward the trees. She could hear the bots calling in the location for reinforcements as they pursued. They cleared the field and entered the forest, but S.W.A.R.M. was closing the gap. As she ran, Rolf called out to his mother, who could be heard in the distance calling desperately to him.

"Jeg elsker deg! Jeg elsker deg!" She cried over and over as her son ran with Nora deeper into the forest. Rolf was crying, but he kept running. Nora lessened her grip on his wrist.

"I'm sorry," she shouted to him, having decided to put a gap between her and the boy. If he fell behind, S.W.A.R.M. would grab him and might slow its pursuit.

Yet, he kept pace. And Nora ran harder. The lights from S.W.A.R.M allowed her to maneuver better, enabling her to increase the gap. After a short time, Rolf finally started to fall behind. As she looked back at him though, she fell. She had come to a ledge, and ran straight off it without knowing. She tumbled down a steep hill, gaining momentum, scrapes and bruises along the way, before she splashed down in a river. The water was freezing, and fast moving. She struggled to keep her head above water as the current quickly moved her along. She couldn't see anything, and only heard the fierce rush of the water as she was slammed into rock after rock. She managed to get her feet in front of her, but the power of the river was too great, and she couldn't swim to the bank or grab a hold of something to stop herself. She drifted away from S.W.A.R.M., and into the dark world, the cold river taking its toll.

It wasn't long before she started to shiver and shut down. She floated along helplessly as the early stages of hypothermia took hold. The current began to slow, but it didn't matter. She couldn't move. She couldn't do anything to save herself. Just before she slipped into unconsciousness, she felt a pair of hands grip her rib cage and pull her toward the riverbank. She tried to see who it was but couldn't tell if the cold hands fishing her from the river belonged to S.W.A.R.M. or not. Then she heard a voice.

"Det er greit."

Nora managed to open her eyes. She saw the boy, Rolf, soaked, sitting next to her. In the faintest voice, she tried to speak, but passed out before she could mutter any words.

39

A trip to the QuestCorp Lunar Command Base at Moon City was an event, regardless of the cause. The city was a series of large spherical buildings interconnected by long, glass corridors. Looming above it were the massive storage tanks of harvested hydrogen, as well as hydrogen that was ready for shipment to Earth. The shuttle reached the landing area, and Armstrong landed it vertically as if making just another routine landing, though he maintained radio silence, even after the base hailed the shuttle repeatedly. Nolan was looking out a window of the shuttle at the moonscape as it landed, awestruck by the sight. Elena came over and sat down next to him.

"Thanks again, Nolan. Thanks for saving Edward. I thought I could get him safely to the shuttle. S.W.A.R.M. moved so fast. I couldn't—"

"—you're welcome. You were incredible in the fight.'

Elena smiled at Nolan, and then looked out the shuttle window. "It's impressive," she said. "Harvesting the Sun, I mean, and turning it into something really good. It's one thing to be proud of. Sometimes I am still in awe that it is even possible. It takes all of this." Elena pointed out the window to all the buildings and storage tanks. "Countless people and mechanical things working around the clock to manage the largest energy production facility ever built. It's sad that Eli wants to take everyone away. He really created something here. Why not use what we have, and save the next planet for a time when there truly is nothing left here for us?"

"Elena, there is nothing left."

Once again, Nolan's thoughts about Earth didn't sit well with Elena.

"Not true. Not true. We can rebuild. Did you know that there is a farm here in Moon City? Crops, livestock. A hydroponic farm with fish too. We could bring them all back to Earth if the cloud was gone. Start over with whatever we have."

Nolan just listened; until they reached the ICS, he didn't want to let Edward or Elena think their hopes were futile. He changed the subject of conversation but tried to acknowledge Elena's hopeful mood.

"I have great memories of growing up on Earth: my parents, the farm, my friends. It all seems so far removed now that it makes me a little homesick."

"Earth wasn't a bad place for you to wind up."

"I can't imagine living anywhere else."

Elena smiled, and looked out the window as the conversation drifted off. Nolan also went back to looking out the window as the shuttle connected to the docking station, but Armstrong soon called out to him. "It took the Apollo mission three days to reach the Moon. It took us less than a day! I took a longer flight to Australia once."

"It's impressive. I never really had the patience for long flights."

Armstrong let out a hardy laugh. "Said the only man who can zap himself anywhere in an instant." He was in good spirits.

Nolan noticed Edward was quiet.

"So, what do you think about this operation, Edward? Mining the Sun, I mean. It's all so revolutionary and new. Are there any consequences to it?"

The doctor answered, high strung on technicalities and nuances. "It's more like farming than mining. No one goes to the Sun to dig up hydrogen; a specially calibrated laser siphons it off, and it's safer than any sort of fuel extraction from Earth. I imagine that whatever consequences occur in space wouldn't mean much of anything to anyone living on Earth, even before the cloud.

To be honest, I am more concerned with the impact here on the Moon, or at least to the people here anyway. The amount of hydrogen stored here would literally blow the Moon to pieces if there was ever an accident."

Nolan hadn't considered this. "Good to know, Doctor. Thanks."

"Don't worry, Nolan. Eli has numerous security measures to prevent such an event."

As the two spoke, the flight crew walked back to the passenger seating area. "We're docked," Armstrong said. "We'll have an hour or so before the Helios is ready for departure. I radioed in. There was no mention of anything out of the ordinary. Either Eli didn't send a message to them, or it's in delay. You all should stretch your legs or get some chow, but stay alert."

"Thank you, Commander," Nolan said. "Will you be piloting the ship to Venus as well?"

"Yes, I will, and I'll have my crew with me as well." He gestured to the crew. "This is Margot Raincloud and Debbie Sands. Hopefully the opposition and solar winds will work out in our favor. An unscheduled flight like this needs some charting. Sands will be crunching the numbers while Margot and I run flight prep."

Nolan patted Armstrong on the shoulder. "Thanks, Joe. Any word on Briggs and Hutchins?"

Armstrong pursed his lips and shook his head.

"I'm sorry," Nolan said. "I'm sure they're alright."

"I hope so," Armstrong said, and then went back to the cockpit.

Nolan turned to Elena. "What should we expect from security forces here? Surely Eli did, or will, alert the base about us hijacking the shuttle."

"Inside the base is a security force. It's like a police force back on Earth; all human, no robots." Armstrong, you're sure there been any chatter on the radio?"

Armstrong just shook his head, focused on his work in the cockpit.

"Well, let's be prepared for an ambush then," Elena said. "Stay alert and try to go unnoticed."

"Got it," Nolan said, then went to join Armstrong. "These are unusual times, Commander. Thank you for helping us." He then extended his hand.

Armstrong, a fit man, gave a very firm handshake. "Happy to help. It's a shame what's happening back on Earth." He then winked at Nolan.

Nolan and the scientists began to ready themselves to exit the ship. Armstrong ordered the flight crew off the shuttle ahead of them, so they could begin preparations on the Helios, which was docked nearby.

When Nolan, Edward, and Elena exited the shuttle they walked into a long corridor lined with windows. Sunlight poured in. It caught them all off guard, and each took their own moment appreciating it. Nolan saw Earth out in the distance but could hardly recognize it. It looked like a lifeless gas planet. As he looked on his mind was flooded with memories of growing up on the farm with his parents. He stifled his thoughts though, so he could focus on what had to be done: get to the control station and confront an enemy in the fourth dimension that he'd never met. To do this, he'd have to quickly find Wu, whom he'd never met either.

As the group walked along the corridor toward the base, Nolan felt the Sun on his skin through the windows. He stopped and turned toward it, but Elena disrupted his bliss.

"Are you alright?"

Turning to her, Nolan answered. "Yes. I didn't realize how much I missed it. You should all go ahead. I'll meet you at the Helios in a little while."

Elena playfully glared at Nolan, as if contemplating what was going through his mind. She cracked a small smile at him. "Try to keep a low profile. I can't imagine anyone here is happy with what is going on down there, but I still don't want to get caught. I'm going to go see if I can speed along prep on the ship. The sooner we leave the better." She turned to catch up with Edward, who was walking ahead.

When they were out of view Nolan smiled, glancing back into the barren wilderness of the Moon before he looked for a door that would let him outside. Once he found it, he took a deep breath, and leaped out into the Moon's atmosphere.

The effects of the Moon's lower gravity were astounding. It was as though every atom in his body was enhanced, strengthened to the point that it shook away the feelings of mortality that had held him back ever since Eli unleashed the radioactive cloud. He jumped up, the strength in his legs pushing him so high off the ground it was as if he was flying above Moon City, allowing him to see the full size and spectrum of the lunar base. The hydrogen tanks were ten stories high, and wider than a football arena. All over the base, an army of menial robots were at work monitoring the buildings, cleaning the windows and surveying the surrounding landscape. None of them resembled S.W.A.R.M., nor did any of them notice him as he hovered above the base. Nolan landed, and then jumped up again. A little further away, other robots, bigger and more industrial looking, were at work carting large shipping containers from a depot near the hydrogen tanks to the shuttle landing bay, where the containers were being prepped for loading. Drifting too close to the storage tanks, Nolan set off a host of alarms. The acute security sensory array that scanned Moon City for meteor threats was tight, quick, and accurate. Red laser lights started to beam into the air from the ground, roaming and searching the sky close to him before quickly zeroing in on him, covering him in red dots. Nolan traced the lasers back to their source, and upon seeing their point of origin realized that things were about to get bad.

Four large robots, the biggest he had ever seen, approached him at breakneck speeds. These ultra-weaponized machines held an attack formation and looked capable enough to do some real damage. He knew that if their operating systems were anything like S.W.A.R.M. he'd be dealing with a strike force capable of real-time chaos. He couldn't risk that considering his proximity to all the harvested hydrogen, so he teleported out into the open plains of the Moon.

By the time he spotted them following him away from the base, they were in formation, and closing in on him. Highly maneuverable and armed with plasma cannons as big as him, they had large mechanical claws that looked like they could easily crush rock. They wasted no time firing shots, and their aim was dead on. In very little time they reached him. Nolan couldn't counter-maneuver. When one finally grabbed him and clamped down, the pressure was like nothing he'd ever felt before. If he teleported away he would only drag the massive robot along if it was touching him in any way. By flexing, writhing, pushing, and pulling, he was finally able to break its hold, but not long enough to charge and jolt away. It took every bit of extra strength he felt from being on the Moon to fight these robots, however, before he could put any distance between him and them, he was clamped down on again, and pinned in place while a large robotic claw squeezed and compounded the pressure. Escape was his only practical option to get the robots to stand down, considering despite their onslaught they were indeed a necessary defense system for the largest bomb ever made. And he had to do it before he ran out of breath.

Spotting a gully a few hundred yards from the base, Nolan decided to take the battle low, hoping the robots would be less agile. He broke free, and as soon as he got his feet onto the Moon's surface, made a beeline of teleportation jumps along the lunar surface toward the gully, sporadically weaving along the way, trying to dodge the relentless plasma charges. The robots moved into an attack formation that allowed them to continue flying, hovering just above him and the ground, just far enough away to stay out of their own blast zones. A plasma charge hit him in the back, sending him flying off his feet and into a rolling tumble along the ground. Luckily, it wasn't Elijum. As he tried to get his eyes fixed on the robots he felt the full weight of one of them land on top of him, pushing him down into the surface and covering him with rocks and Moon dust. Pinned, he had the quick thought of burrowing himself into the ground beneath the robots. His tremendous strength made it possible for him to punch and move through the Moon's subsurface, so he dug down deep enough that the heat sensors used by the robots could not register his signature. The robots continued to survey the battlefield as Nolan burrowed his way back to the base completely undetected.

When he got back to the base he immediately exhaled before taking in a huge breath of fresh air. He looked out the window toward the robots, which were now blasting into the hole through which he escaped. At the same time, he noticed an assortment of alarms and automated messages sounding off emergency warnings in loops over the base's intercom. The base was entering lockdown. As he gained his bearings, he saw Elena and Edward running toward him. Elena shouted as she ran toward him.

"Get to the Helios! You've been spotted! We need to fly now!"

"What about Wu?" Nolan shouted while running at their pace.

"He's on the ship. Armstrong knew where to find him," Elena answered. As they ran, Edward tripped, but was caught by Elena who righted him and kept them moving without slowing down.

Nolan ran with the scientists to the Helios, and once they boarded, Elena yelled to Armstrong to take off. As the ship left the ground, dozens of red lasers scanned its hull. Recognizing the vessel, the defense system stood down. Nolan looked through a window and saw the defense robots still out on the moonscape, searching near where he had escaped from them. The ship lifted quickly away from the Moon and set off toward Venus, deploying its large sails to catch the solar winds as it entered open space.

40

Warnings were flashing on the monitors of Eli's control room. He looked and saw S.W.A.R.M. mobilizing on one of the screens. He heard gunfire but couldn't see where it was coming form. A sudden explosion shook the facility. "Eliminate the threat by any means necessary."

"*Affirmative.*"

He looked across his screens to try and spot where the raiders were launching their attack from. It was a new position, somewhere not heavily watched, so it didn't show in any of the monitors. On screen, S.W.A.R.M. began moving toward the west wall of the facility in droves. More gunfire ensued. Heavy fire sprayed into the robot legion, dropping units fast. Eli watched as a monitor showed robot after robot going offline. Smoke and dust from the explosion made it difficult to see anything through the video monitors. Eli moved to another station nearby and hit a switch. The monitor screen blinked on with a live camera feed of a small landing pad. He grabbed a control at the desk and began to manipulate it. The view in the monitor shifted up as he started to fly a surveillance drone toward the fight. Hovering in over the fray, Eli moved the drone past the position held by S.W.A.R.M. and halted it just over the wall. He saw a group of soldiers set up with a half dozen .50 caliber machine guns mounted in truck beds spraying bullets into his robot forces.

S.W.A.R.M. was firing back, but the trucks had sheets of metal welded to them. The large guns were gunning down the horde faster than it could advance.

"Retreat," Eli commanded. "Secure cover."

"*Affirmative.*"

Eli watched his robot legion break the line and scatter into the facility. As they retreated the gunfire followed, picking off units one by one. Eli hadn't seen an attack like this before from any of the raiding bands that had attempted to breach the facility. And with Savior gone, the facility had no defense for the attack other than S.W.A.R.M. All Eli could do was watch from the control room.

Once inside the facility, however, S.W.A.R.M. performed. Under cover they were able to formulate a more strategic defense, and kept the big guns from advancing through the hole left in the wall from the explosion. Glancing in another monitor, Eli saw a small armed group enter the facility at the front gate, which was left unguarded due to the major onslaught underway. The group moved into the facility stealthily and tactically, like a specials teams force would.

"Hostiles entering at the gate. Pursue."

"*Affirmative.*"

As Eli watched, he saw that S.W.A.R.M. could not successfully peel off from the main fighting to pursue the small team. The cover fire was too heavy, and the handful of robots that attempted to break off were quickly gunned down. Eli kept eyes on the small group of raiders as they swiftly moved into the facility, showing in one monitor screen and then another as they advanced. They were headed toward the interior building, where Eli's control room was. Seeing this, Eli stepped away from the monitors and went to a cage mounted on the wall that held some artillery. He grabbed and loaded a handgun and placed it into his belt before grabbing a semiautomatic rifle and several magazines. He headed back to the monitors. S.W.A.R.M. was still pinned down, and the small group had made it into the interior building. Eli turned toward the door and aimed his rifle.

It wasn't long before an explosion blew the door open, sending debris into Eli along with a shockwave from the blast. It knocked him violently to the floor. Stunned, he hadn't even tried to move before he felt hands grab him and pin his arms behind his back with restraints. He was picked up from the floor and dropped into his chair.

Eight men in tactical gear and masks stood in front of him. Somewhat dazed, he tried to speak. One of the men spoke instead. "Tell S.W.A.R.M. to stand down." Eli just looked at the man. The man struck him in the face with the butt of his rifle. Eli fell to the ground, bleeding from his mouth. The man spoke again. "TELL THEM TO STAND DOWN!" He then picked up the comm from a control desk and threw it at Eli. Eli rolled onto his side and grabbed the comm with his tied hands. He switched it on and gave the order. The gunfire quickly ceased.

Eli looked around and saw several of the men move into the control room to various stations. The man who struck him kneeled next to him. "We don't want to destroy your robots. We just want what you've got."

Eli looked firmly at the man. "You can't have it," he said.

The man laughed, but turned serious when he spoke again. "I'm going to explain this once because I'm not very patient." As he spoke, Eli noticed in a monitor that the trucks with guns were moving into the facility through the hole in the wall. The man continued. "I want this facility. I want all your guns. All your food. I'm going to run things here, and you're going to make sure I get everything I need."

"What makes you think you can pull that off?"

"Well, I've got you, which means I've got your voice, which means I've got S.W.A.R.M. See? I know how it all works. I've *got* you." The man started to laugh again. He gestured for his crew to join in.

Eli started to laugh as well, the man looking at him with a puzzled look as he did.

"Why is that funny to you?" He asked.

"Spitfire," Eli said. Instantly, several guns on turrets lowered from the ceiling and shot the men. They all dropped to the floor, the man who was speaking to Eli landing right beside him, the puzzled look still on his face. Eli then looked in the monitor and saw all the trucks with the .50 caliber guns surrounded by his S.W.A.R.M. force. He grabbed the comm that was thrown at him earlier.

"Identify targets."

"Identifying. Targets acquired."

"Swarm."

"Affirmative."

Eli watched with a look of gratification as the remaining robots of his legion descended on the men.

41

Nolan entered Wu's quarters on the ship. Wu was sitting on the bed, feet on the floor, eyes facing the door. He didn't move or speak when Nolan entered. He looked like a sick old man. A wheelchair was near his bed. Other than a twitch in his hands and fingers and very shallow breaths, he showed no signs of life. Nolan stared at him, somewhat caught off guard at the sight. Wu began to speak to Nolan in a gravelly whisper.

"I know who you are," he said, a soft chuckle coming out as he spoke. Wu gestured by lifting a hand, but didn't point or have any other purpose to his movement.

"Edward maybe told you that I am mad; that I am blind. Half true." Wu laughed louder and shook his head. "I am not blind. I can no longer see, but in another dimension, I can see just fine." His laughter continued. "I can see you too." Wu turned his head and looked directly at Nolan. He stared, and then pointed at him for an awkward length of time.

"It's nice to meet you, Doctor Wu. I am sorry for the trauma you've endured."

Wu continued. "There is something in you that I can see, but cannot understand. This is how I know you must be Savior walking into my room. Sit with me."

Nolan walked a chair over to Wu and sat next to the bed.

"Doctor, please, call me Nolan."

Wu laughed some more. "Thank you, Nolan. Nolan from space. Nolan the spaceman with the spaceman's ship."

"Doctor, I am going to face whatever it is that attacked you. Is there anything you can tell me about it?"

"Nolan. No-lan. No-lan the space-man. More laughter. "My own doing, No-lan, my own fault, but I waste no time being sorry about it. I was once brilliant, but I played with forces I did not understand and paid heavily for it. But, better me, or better yet, you."

"Eli Quest wants to send everyone on Earth through a wormhole to a new planet. We need to access the wormhole cache. What did you experience when you visited it in the fourth dimension?"

An odd smirk came over Wu's face. He nodded as if he had just heard something he agreed with. "I opened a door and walked inside to see if I could find what I was looking for. Keys to the universe I never found." Wu burst out laughing.

"What did you see, Doctor? What was there in the fourth dimension when you went in?"

Wu continued to chuckle while he answered. "The fourth dimension, of course." He smiled subtly, and with a slight grimace, he continued. "The door I opened was not meant to open. It changed me in the same way it has changed you."

"I'm sorry, Doctor, I don't understand."

"Space isn't all there is. What you see is only what you see, but there is so much more than just that. Humans cannot even see the fourth dimension except for where it crosses with our dimension, but even then, you wouldn't know what you were looking at or that it was another dimension at all. When I went inside of it, it went inside of me. Every part of my being and my body blended with the dimension. The dimension occupied the same space as my eyes along with the space in which my eyes see. After that, my ability to see changed altogether, so that now all I can see is where the fourth dimension touches ours." Wu then leaned toward Nolan with a big smile on his face. "I can see the fourth dimension in you, No-lan, which makes me believe that you too have been to the fourth dimension."

"Doctor Wu, I'm sorry, but I have spent my whole life here on Earth."

Wu's face and demeanor relaxed. "Interesting." He paused before he continued. "Yet, it is here with you. Within you. You have its traits, and yet you don't. LIKE A MUTT!" Wu laughed loudly, and for a good while. "Do you know about where you came from?"

"The only information I have about my home world came from data my parents recorded about the planet and its destruction, in a language I don't understand. I don't know anything about my kind or my parents other than some images from their escape."

"Eli showed you. I've seen it too. Such a lovely planet."

Nolan sat quietly. The doctor wasn't as scrambled as he had expected, but wasn't all that helpful either. Wu eventually filled the silence. "Have you ever seen Venus?"

"No, I haven't."

"You should. It's beautiful. But, not with Edward."

Nolan was puzzled. "Doctor?"

"The cache is haunted. The ghost there ... its thoughts mixed in with mine, as though our minds shared the same space or energy. But the thoughts weren't…good." Wu sighed. "We crossed a line when we inserted the cache into its dimension."

"Ghost? Do you mean the forces that harmed you?"

Wu nodded. "If you go there, be ready to fight."

"Doctor Wu, do you think it was a being that hurt you, or was it the dimension in general?"

"I don't know. I never believed in ghosts before," Wu said, in a whimsical way. "It is beyond my understanding. You must cross into the fourth dimension and see for yourself. But it will be there. Waiting, and mad!" Wu tried to suppress his laughter.

"You think it is a sentient being. Do you think it is looking for revenge? Mad because we invaded its space?" Nolan asked.

"Yes. Mad. Invaded by an inferior being from an inferior dimension. I believe it could do everything to our dimension that it did to me, if it felt so inclined." Wu trailed off into a laughing spell that didn't stop.

Nolan decided to end the conversation. Wu was peculiar, understandably so, but Nolan wasn't in the mood for laughs. "Thank you, Doctor," he said as he left the room, Wu still laughing outrageously.

42

The trip to Venus took just under a month. Solar wind speeds carried the ship along quickly, as the course between Earth and its sister planet was optimal. Nolan often stepped outside of the ship to ride along on the masts of the solar sails, taking in the full view of everything space could offer as the ship made its way through the inner solar system. The experience invigorated him. As he sat on the mast, his mind took him back to a memory of his father, Frank Keller.

Nolan sat with Frank on the tailgate of a pickup truck near where the crop fields and the backyard of the farmhouse met. Nolan's head only reached as high as Frank's shoulder as they sat side by side. Dirt from the good day's work clung to the sweat on their skin and they enjoyed the cooling air coming in with the midsummer night. "Son, look there," Frank said, pointing to the crops. "There are two things that matter to those crops. Sunshine and rain. The soil is important; it holds the plants to the ground and keeps them steady in the wind, but without sunshine and rain, they won't grow." Frank looked at Nolan who sat quietly, listening intently. A smile came across his face. He continued. "It's how everything should work, Nolan. Sunshine and rain don't come from the same place. They don't come around at the same time usually either, yet they work together to make something better than themselves. I know you've learned the science behind it all in school, but the fact that it somehow all comes together has always amazed me. I've always been proud that our little piece of the Earth turns out food year after year thanks to a lot of sweat and a little love from Mother Nature. I always hoped one day I'd have a son to take over for me and be proud of it too."

"I will, Dad."

"Well, I appreciate hearing that, son, but we both know you might set out one day for something more. I want you to know that I'm okay with that. This gift of yours, this strength that you have, will serve you well in more ways than the farm ever could. Don't hold on here if you see a chance to make something better than yourself somewhere else. Your mother and I are proud of you, Nolan. Despite the advantages you have, you show your heart to the people around you every day. Keep that part of yourself. Don't let the world take it from you. Lord knows it will try." Frank's gaze drifted off into the distance.

"I will, Dad. Don't worry. I won't hurt anyone. I promised. I won't."

"I know, son. I know you won't. Just remember what I said though. You are great, so be great. We're behind you all the way, even if you can't see us rooting for you."

Edward's voice came out over the ship's exterior comm and interrupted Nolan's thoughts.

"Unless you have some anaerobic capabilities that we are not aware of, you should come in. You can't hold your breath all the way to Venus."

Nolan smirked, took in one last look of the cosmos, and then moved from the mast to the bay doors to reenter the ship. Once inside, he was met by Edward. The mood was light, and the two began to banter.

"I need to practice," Nolan said. "As long as you don't lock me out I'll be fine."

"You are remarkable, Nolan. I would really love to do a study when this is all over."

"I know. You've said that quite a few times since we left."

"I feel bad in knowing this, now that I know you, but when we studied your mother's remains we discovered how remarkable her anatomy was."

Nolan's good mood lessened. "I don't know that I want to hear the details, Doctor."

"No, no. Of course not. But, in broad terms, you and your mother are nothing like the rest of us on a cellular level. Your cell walls are nearly impenetrable, except under exposure to—"

"—Radioactive clouds, yes, I am aware. So, what do I need to know once we get to Venus? Are there security measures to face like the ones in Moon City?"

Edward paused, and then nodded empathetically. "No. Nothing like that. There is an array in place that monitors meteors and asteroids, but no robot automation. You should be fine. As long as you don't do anything to make the defense system think you are a meteor."

"Okay. What about the cache and the '4D Man'?"

Edward's face drooped as though the heaviness of the conversation was weighing it down. "I've told you everything I know. Wu said it was a man?"

"I think so. I'm not sure, really."

"I don't know if things will be any different for you than they were for him. Do you think you can really clear it, or him, from the cache?"

Nolan contemplatively looked out the ship's portal, out into the darkness of space, before answering. "You need to be able to open wormholes again. Can you get that done?"

Edward sighed, and then nodded. A frown came over his face. "Things were good before the cache, Nolan. For all of us. We really were a remarkable team. Elena and Arthur were the two most fortunate humans in the universe. They routinely traveled through the wormholes for harvesting missions, and Wu and I sorted out the science and engineering." Edward smiled while he drifted into a daydream state. "I loved hearing their stories about what they had seen even more than seeing the photos of it all. Their stories were filled with a passion and awe that was almost juvenile. Wondrous tales of the universe. We agreed to not visit any planets identified as habitable by reconnaissance probes, and would altogether skip any solar system with civilizations on any of the planetary surfaces, and we still discovered so much. Even though harvesting was always the mission, mapping the universe as we went along was a far more astonishing and rewarding task in itself."

"I can only imagine, Doctor. It sounds truly amazing," Nolan said flatly.

"Harvesting missions held their own level of excitement too. Elena managed the Harvester while Arthur collected data readings from the solar systems they visited, and then mapped 3D models for the QuestCorp database. They collected information that covered data on solar system geography, composition, life spectrum, and sun type. QuestCorp used the information to run comparative diagnostics to better identify similarities between systems and harvests in order to improve site selection for future harvesting missions, but we just loved the science of it." Edward looked at Nolan squarely so that they stood eye to eye. "I know what the universe is capable of, Nolan. I know what can be found out there, and I know what can come of it. Have faith in me. I will cure Earth."

Nolan still wasn't interested in Edward's plea.

Margot entered the room, which broke the tension. The flight duration had allowed her to become jovial and relaxed around Nolan. "Sitting outside again? I'm really starting to think you don't like any of us in here."

Nolan laughed. "Just enjoying the ride and clearing my head."

"A man like you must have a lot to think about."

"You have no idea."

"Saying that to a military woman could get you hurt. I've been on many high stakes missions. But everyone on Earth is counting on *you* right now, whether they know it or not."

Edward glared at Nolan with a look of vindication on his face. Nolan ignored him.

"I want to tell you a story," Margot said, sitting down in a chair across from Nolan. She gestured for him to sit as well. "I am very tied to Earth. I am Haida; Native

American. I belong to my ancestors in the north who all belong to the lands there. They lived their life there in the light, and in the dark. We have a story about the beginning, when the world was covered in darkness, just like it is now. In that time, a raven, cunning and wise, and tired of living in a world he could not see, learned of a man with a great treasure. This man held all the light in the universe in a box. The raven set out to find this man, and in finding him asked to see the light. The man would not let him, so the raven thought of a way to see the light. The old man had a daughter, and one day the raven transformed himself and hid in the daughter's drinking water. When the daughter drank the water, the raven slid down into her belly, and transformed again into a child. When this ravenchild was born he was loved by his mother and grandfather. In time, the ravenchild convinced his grandfather to show him the light inside the box. When the old man opened the box, the ravenchild stole the light, and flew away with it. This is how light began."

Nolan listened to Margot's story respectfully but was unconvinced that anything could change. "Margot, that's a great story, but we're not here to bring back the light."

Edward scoffed.

Margot smiled, and chuckled. "Nolan, you *are* the ravenchild. You are here to bring the light back." Nolan turned and looked out the ship's portal. Margot looked at Nolan, and then shrugged off his disinterest. "It's a long flight. Think about it," she said, before leaving him and Edward to resume their discussion.

Nolan turned to Edward and spoke before Edward could get a word out. "I think I'm going to turn in for a while."

"And I think I'm going to stay up for a while."

Nolan shook his head and then walked over to a bunk just off the common area and stretched out in it. Edward left the common area altogether. Nolan laid for a while, restless with his thoughts. He had made the choice to help Eli instead of Edward, leaving a whole planet to die, but that didn't mean it sat well with him.

As he tried to fall asleep he heard a familiar voice speaking over an intercom in Wu's room, which was nearby. He recognized the voice as Eli's. Nolan listened in.

"How are you, Chris?"

"Eli! Hello." The standard laughter accompanied Wu's conversation. "We are headed to Venus."

"Is everyone on board with the plan?"

"Trust in Savior. He can do what needs to be done. I can see it in him."

"I trust you, Chris. Just don't get too attached to the alien."

"He's a good man, Elijah."

"He's not a man. You above everyone else knows this. He's a freak."

"You shouldn't leave him behind."

"I won't have this discussion, Chris."

"If you leave him, leave me too."

"Just execute the plan."

Wu laughed like a madman before answering. "Fundraiser, you don't call the shots here. You are at the mercy of the people on this ship. We will decide what to do. Not you."

"Chris, this isn't optional. If you won't do it, I will. Arthur gave me his access codes. I can now control the whole base from here. The alien doesn't come back."

"A bluff! Arthur would never do that."

"I have been patient with you, Chris. Your recovery and current demeanor has been trying, to put it lightly, but as we get closer to our new beginning people are more readily proving to be disposable. I'd hate to see that be the case for you, but I have no tolerance for any more deviations. Complete the mission."

Wu answered in a somber tone. "Do it yourself." Wu began his laughter. "You can't."

"Goodbye, Chris. I hope to see you again."

Eli ended the call. Nolan could hear Wu cursing under his breath.

He listened as Wu stirred for a while, eventually finding his way to sleep. Nolan rolled over and closed his eyes to fall asleep as well.

43

Eli was waiting just off the shuttle's landing pad as it made its landing in the facility. His foot tapped restlessly on the ground and his face was drawn as he waited impatiently for the ship to land. He greeted his software specialist, Diya Patel, when she exited the shuttle.

"Uh, hello, Mister Quest," she said, caught off guard. "I wasn't expecting to see you here."

"Is the upgrade ready?"

"Yes, sir. It is."

"Follow me."

He led her to a small, utilitarian office just off the landing field. There was a large computer mainframe in it that looked out of place.

"Everything you need is here." He gestured to a chair at the computer. "Please get started," he said, sitting in a chair next to her.

Diya sat, pulled out a disk from an attaché case she brought in, and inserted it into the computer.

"How long will it take?" Eli asked.

"Our network in Moon City is much faster. It could take hours down here."

Eli's brow lowered. "What can I expect from the upgrade? How much more efficient will S.W.A.R.M. be?"

"It will direct itself."

"It already does."

"I mean it will be more capable of making its own decisions. Specifically, it won't do something you tell it to do if it detects your commands are coerced. It will read your command and then decide if it should follow, instead of just following. Autonomous verses semi-autonomous."

Eli pursed his lips, and hesitated. "I trust your work, Diya."

"Thank you. I am also installing a speech upgrade. It will speak more like we do."

"No more 'affirmative'?"

"No, sir. As requested."

"Good work. Do what you can to speed up the upgrade. I'll leave you here to finish it up. Catch the first available flight to Moon City once you're done. Bring two units with you. I'll see you there." Eli left the small office, and entered the shuttle, which departed immediately.

44

When the team entered orbit above Venus, the Interstellar Control Station quickly came into view. It was unimpressive; a station shaped like an old toy top floating in space. The docking station extended like an arm, and already had two smaller ships docked in the bays.

"What ship is that?" Nolan asked, pointing at one of the ships through a porthole in the common quarters of the Helios.

Elena, resting, looked through another porthole as they sailed closer to the control station. "That is the Harvester; the original machine that QuestCorp started its interstellar mining operation with. She's the one that's seen all the action."

"It was your ship?"

"Yes, my baby. I'm not lying when I tell you I've been all over the universe in that ship. It's good to see her again."

Nolan saw the warm feelings Elena had for the ship. "Why was it left here? It seems like an invaluable machine."

"It is. It's one of a kind, and no ship has done what she has, but after Chris was injured, Eli called us all back to Moon City, leaving the station abandoned. When we left we had to leave everything as it was."

"Why Moon City?"

"Eli was launching the Demeter Initiative and wanted us there. We didn't know what it was going to turn out to be at the time. He tricked us. We should have known better."

Nolan didn't bother to feign any sympathy. "That's hard to believe. You reconstructed raw materials from another galaxy so that it would bond with ozone. What did you think you were doing?"

"Helping. Eli was always innovating ways to make the world a better place. I thought he was looking for a way to increase the ozone layer's effectiveness. I knew he wanted to take people to the new world, but I didn't know he was taking *everyone*, and not in the manner he went about doing it. We never would've helped had we—"

Edward interrupted, barging into the common quarters, filled with energy and excitement. "Alright. We have work to do now, and it's time to get things in order! Doctor Wu, once we are aboard the station we'll need you to find and access any overrides there might be in the system controls. Try to figure out how Chance reconfigured all the passcodes and entry points. Elena, you and Nolan will have to ready the Harvester. Hopefully, its power core is in good shape. I need to find Chance's maps in the database and start plotting the wormhole coordinates for Earth."

Wu, who had been resting on a bed just off the common quarters, raised his arm and gave Edward a thumbs up. Nolan looked noticeably impressed.

"What? What is it?" Edward asked.

"Nothing. Let's get to it."

"Yes, well, while you all 'get to it' I will be looking through data for an element that we can introduce to Earth's atmosphere that is strong enough to pull the cloud's bonded molecules apart right there in the sky. We found the bulk of what we harvested in a huge asteroid belt created by Oua. I think we should start there. Perhaps the large concentration there is a result of some force of attraction."

"You're talking about my destroyed homeworld," Nolan said, his eyes fixed on Edward.

Edward's face dropped, and his eyes widened. He stammered in finding the right thing to say. "Yes. I am. I'm sorry, but I was just thinking out—"

"—ENOUGH!"

Edward, with an air of confusion and concern, leaned back until he felt the wall with his shoulder, and then slid down to the bench seat that was behind him. Nolan continued.

"I am going to clear the cache of whatever is haunting it, and you are going to assist Doctor Wu in opening the wormhole Eli needs. If I fail, you are going to help Doctor Wu destroy the cache, and all the wormholes in it, and then recreate the wormhole that Eli needs. Doctor Wu is leading this mission once I go into the fourth dimension."

Wu chuckled in the background. Edward's eyes began to well up a little as he looked at Nolan in disbelief. Quickly, he looked to Elena, who also had a look of shock on her face. Nolan paused as the two sat silently, staring at one another with varied looks of panic and sadness.

"Edward, you have no real science demonstrating how an ionized cloud stuck in the sky can be removed, or even neutralized. Give up your hope and focus on the plan. Eli and I are in agreement."

Elena jumped in before Edward could. "Nolan, how can you say such a thing? You have been hope to so many. You've saved the day literally hundreds of times! How can you give up on Edward now when he is so close to a chance at saving everything?"

"Elena, I'm not giving up. I want to save the world, just like you, but let's compare our actions. I have saved countless people. You helped destroy the planet. Your judgment is poor, and your choices devastating. *I* say we are going with Eli on this."

Feeling betrayed, Elena bluntly continued with Nolan. "But you'll die, and so will Earth. Do you even care?!"

"I do. But worlds die. I want to make sure the people live."

Edward, sitting on the bench with his elbows on his knees and face in his hands, was overcome by his emotions. "You are a bastard. You tricked us. You waited until you were as strong as ever to tell us you've been stringing us along this whole time. You're going to let an entire planet die even though I can save it."

"I've been clear all along that I was helping Eli. You were misled by your own hopes and theories. We go with Eli's plan. End of story."

Elena placed her hand on Nolan's arm gently. "Nolan, trust Edward to do his job. We trusted you to do yours, and you have. You got us here. We are all capable of success on this mission in our own ways. This isn't just you, remember?"

"We are here because I told Eli I would get you here. I told him when we reached Venus I would clear the cache and Edward would open the wormhole for the people. Now that we are here, I am giving you no choice but to help Eli." Nolan flexed his muscle under Elena's hand, and she quickly let go of his arm. "Let's dock and get to work."

Nolan headed up to the shuttle cockpit to speak with Armstrong, leaving Edward and Elena dumbstruck.

45

Eli was back in Moon City, monitoring the Venus station's signal feed for signs of the Helios' arrival through surveillance cameras and remote system monitors linked to the ICS. There was a great amount of lag in the feed, but it was all he could do, and although he had allowed Nolan to accompany his scientists to Venus, he stewed as he sat and waited. The success of his last resort effort to elevate mankind relied on an alien. It blurred the line between success and failure. Control had left his hands, and this wore at him. Savior was the only person Eli had forbidden from his new and better world but was now the last hope he had of ever seeing it.

Waiting was something he was unaccustomed to, but he endured it much better than he did the slip of control. Speaking in his office to a single S.W.A.R.M. robot now standing in for Nora, Eli issued the orders for Earth's evacuation, gambling on Nolan's success and Wu's ability to open a wormhole.

"Send the transfer crews to the transport shuttles," he said. "I want them on the Earth immediately to prepare the people for evacuation. Send everyone else down as well. Everyone on Moon City is first through the wormhole once it is opened on Earth."

"*Yes, sir.*"

"Load the hydrogen from Tank 1 onto the shuttle and dispatch it. Assign a squadron from Earth to it as well as the factory ships. I want food production to continue, uninterrupted, and I want full operation on the new world without delay. Execute."

"*Should the ships launch before there is a wormhole for passage?*"

The question caught Eli off guard. "Don't wait! Just get it done."

"*Yes, sir.*" The S.W.A.R.M. robot stood motionless for a moment in Eli's office, communicating its orders silently to the horde. *"Orders issued."*

"Go," Eli said.

The robot said nothing and left the room. Eli turned to his desk and sat down, shaking his head. He sat silently for a moment, staring at nothing, and fidgeting with his watch. He called S.W.A.R.M. on the watch.

"Yes?"

"Status report for locating Nora Reinhard."

There was a brief delay in the response. *"Still missing."*

Eli closed his eyes and took in a deep breath that he exhaled slowly. He spoke into the watch again: "Keep looking."

"Yes, sir."

Eli stood up from his desk and turned to the massive window behind him. He looked out at the darkened Earth, which blended with the black backdrop of space.

"I will find you," he said. "Someday you'll thank me."

46

Armstrong's voice rumbled through the Helios' intercom: *"There's damage to the main docking bay. I won't be able to couple with it, and the rest of the dock isn't fitted for this ship. We'll have to spacewalk to the control station. Untethered."*

Nolan and the doctors were in the common quarters when the message came over. The tension between them had made for a quiet and uncomfortable end to their space journey to Venus.

"That won't be a problem," Nolan said. "You all can gear up in spacesuits, and I'll pull you over to the station. It'll be a lot faster that way."

"So, what, now you can fly in space?" Edward asked sarcastically.

"I can push off the Helios and glide over to the control station."

"Well, I'm only a *theorist*, but *theoretically* we can all get over there without your help. We just need one person with a propulsive pack, which we have, to pull us all over.

"Commander Armstrong says there is only one propulsive pack aboard the ship, but they didn't check it in pre-flight. Armstrong can stay on the ship and use its thrusters to counter me pushing off from it. We should get some good momentum in the process."

"All at once then? That's how you see this going? Why not just teleport us over to the station?" Elena asked aggressively.

"I've never tried teleporting someone in space. I don't know if anything will go wrong or not. You can all tether to me. I'll get you there safely."

"We are short a suit, Nolan. You'll have to make two trips. I mean, that's fine, we are in a synchronized orbit with—"

"—I don't need a suit, Elena, I'll be fine. We'll all go together."

Armstrong came over the intercom again: *We are in synchronous orbit with the station. Suit up.* " Armstrong had positioned the shuttle as close as he could to the control station so that the spacewalk would be as short as possible. *"If we get any closer, we might jeopardize the station when we fire thrusters."*

Margot and Debbie entered the common quarters to help the scientists suit up for the spacewalk. As everyone started to move toward the equipment, Wu addressed the imminent mission while it awkwardly hung in the air like a questionable storm on the horizon.

"When we open the hyperspace bridge, we won't be alone. We have one chance."

Nolan added to Wu's advice ahead of Wu's typical laughing spell. "Doctor Wu is right. Everyone needs to stick to their part of the plan no matter what, and no one should go near the cache other than me. Without knowing what we are up against, we must minimize unknowns. Clearing the cache is the priority, so we can open the wormhole. Doctor Wu, Edward, once I have done my part, get to work on yours."

"Whatever you say, *Savior.* You're *the boss.*" Edward answered back snidely. "Tell me, do you have a plan for getting out of the cache if you should get trapped, by the way? Do you even know whether or not that is possible? I happen to know a bit about that sort of thing, so it might be a good idea for you to ask me about it."

"Thank you, Edward, but I don't need you to worry about that right now. Just be ready to fire up the new wormhole if I don't make it back out."

Elena, gearing up, grew visibly upset. "You don't plan on coming out of it," she said to Nolan.

"That's not important," Nolan said. "We're saving lives. Stay focused."

The group suited up in preparation for the spacewalk. Once the suits were pressurized, the scientists, Nolan, and Sands tethered themselves together and exited the ship out into the emptiness of space. Armstrong and Raincloud stayed on the Helios to pilot it during the spacewalk maneuver, and to keep it ready for departure in case of an emergency. Once outside, Nolan planted his feet against the Helios, and pushed off as Armstrong fired the ship's thrusters, pulling the group to the control station. When they reached it, they crashed hard against its doors, but were otherwise okay. Nolan removed the tether connecting him to everyone else and reconnected it to the control station before moving over to the docking bay to open the doors. He had to pry them open with his hands before bringing the group inside. Once everyone was in the station, he forced the doors shut, and the bay began to pressurize. It was a near flawless spacewalk.

Once in the station's control room, everyone fell in line under Elena's direction. She assumed command as if she had never left. Nolan carried Wu to a control desk where he began working to unlock the wormhole cache and bring the wormhole directory online. Eli had sent a braille keyboard in the shuttle with him, along with screen reader software. Sands joined Nolan in the docking bay to help get the Harvester prepped while Edward sat down to review the database and coordinate charts, so he could connect the wormhole to the refugee camp on Earth. Despite the random group of people working together, preparations went well, until alarms started sounding all over the control station.

Initially unaware of what the warning alarms were alerting her to, Elena started to secure the assets of the mission. She ordered Doctor Wu to investigate the source of the alarms and to survey the area surrounding the station for any objects that might be on a collision course with it. She ordered Nolan and Sands away from the Harvester, and once they were clear of it she dumped it from the docking bay, setting it adrift from the station on an autopilot emergency protocol. She radioed Armstrong and ordered him to grab it with Helios' mechanical arm and then move away from the control station. She ordered Edward to get into one of the evacuation pods on the station. Wu traced the source of the warning system's trigger and shut the alarms off, and then pushed himself away from the control desk, wheeling across the control room on a desk chair. He spoke with a tremble in his voice, and fear filled his eyes.

"The cache has been unlocked. All wormholes have been opened, and the hyperspace bridge has materialized."

"What? How?!" Elena asked, panicked and puzzled.

Wu tittered. "I don't know…I don't know, Elena…we must get out of here. Everything is open. We're sitting on the edge of all the corners of our universe and a dimension we can't see. We must go!"

As Nolan listened, he looked out the control room's windows. Outside the control station, a connection between the third and fourth dimensions had materialized out of empty space and bridged the two together. From his conversations with Wu, he knew that anything could move one way or the other through it, or even pass through the dozens of open wormholes in the cache that led all over the third dimension. Edward came running from the evacuation pod, and realizing what was happening, looked to Elena.

"Wu, what is this? Why is this happening?" Nolan asked.

"I don't know. This isn't how the system works. One wormhole is supposed to be opened at a time, and the hyperspace portal to the fourth dimension is only supposed to be opened when we are ready to pass through it."

"What did you do? How did you turn everything on?" Elena asked.

"I didn't. I didn't even find a backdoor to the system before everything just, opened up."

"What does this mean, Doctor Wu? Did we cause this?" Nolan asked.

"I…I don't know," Wu said. "A system failure, or gravitational anomaly, perhaps. A big bang? I really don't know; this is all just too big! We need to shut it down or retreat. The system isn't designed to work like this."

"Shut it down, Wu!" Elena shouted.

"I don't think I can. I suppose, maybe, if I knew how it had opened in the first place I could reverse the sequence, but I'm still locked out of the controls." He started laughing, nervously.

"Concentrate on the wormhole for Earth," Edward said. "Get in and close it as fast as you can. Then we'll worry about the rest."

"Can the cache be opened remotely?" Nolan asked.

"It would have to be, because it wasn't opened here."

"Where else are there controls for the cache?" Nolan asked.

"Here," Wu said working maniacally at his station, "and wherever Eli is, I guess. He said he had access. He wasn't bluffing."

"Entirely possible," Elena said darkly.

"There are no other controls," Edward said. "And Eli would have to dial in here to access these controls if he wanted to remotely operate things here; it's like a local area network. You can't just open it from Earth or Moon City without accessing these controls first, and these controls are still under Chance's locks."

Fearing the worst, Nolan asked Wu the only question left to ask. "Doctor, you have been on the other side. Any chance whatever is in there opened the system from that side?"

Wu stopped his work and looked directly at Nolan. "We can't rule anything out when it comes to the fourth dimension. You need to get out there now."

Amid the confusion of how the system activated and how to deal with it, the Harvester and the shuttle—

now tethered together—were sucked into the fourth dimension through the hyperspace bridge, as if grabbed, disappearing instantly with Armstrong and Raincloud still onboard. Nolan watched as it happened.

"Doctor Wu, try to gain control. I'm going in," Nolan said.

Elena grabbed him by the wrist, staring at him with somber eyes. "Good luck."

"Thanks. Build a new wormhole. Help Eli transport everyone."

"We will."

Wu called out to Nolan. "Nolan. This goes without saying, but you can't let anything cross the hyperspace bridge. Destroy whatever you find in the other dimension."

"I will, Doctor Wu, just do your best to close the bridge behind me. And make sure it doesn't open again."

Wu sat staring out at the hyperspace bridge, the connection between the third and fourth dimension. "Time and space will not be on your side," he told Nolan.

"Got it."

47

As Nolan looked through the hyperspace bridge for a sign of the Helios or the Harvester, Wu's voice came over the comm.

"Nolan, remember that some aspect of you already exists in the fourth dimension. It is possible that it may seem no different to you than our dimension. Good luck."

Nolan heeded the advice. As he floated in space between the control center and the hyperspace bridge linking the two dimensions, he stared with an unfettered grit into the hole of the unknown, and it wasn't long before something stared back. Doctor Wu's hypothesis that he might have an enhanced ability to interact with the fourth dimension was right. His hybrid, multidimensional biology enabled him to understand the sentiment behind the murky image: hatred.

Nolan perceived glimpses of things that resembled facial features, but they were fleeting and irregularly prominent. They seemed to appear in and out of time, as if they were simultaneously a memory and a reality, leaving him with a complex, confusing and disorienting feeling of déjà vu. Appendages manifested and vanished in the same space and moment. It seemed much larger than him, but without being able to clearly define the surrounding space it was impossible to gauge how truly large it was.

Nolan could read the enemy emotionally, and he felt oddly linked to it, as if he shared thoughts with it. He immediately became aware that his enemy was enraged by the cache having been inserted into its home and had willingly chosen this moment to unleash its fury. The being writhed in insuppressible feelings of revenge, punishment, and destruction. Nolan tried to reveal his thoughts to the being as well in an attempt to reason with it, but his opponent set the terms.

It reached out with indiscernible momentum and grabbed Nolan, dragging him through the hyperspace bridge and into the fourth dimension. Nolan had to scramble to adapt. Once in the foreign dimension, he quickly saw that the dimension itself was no different than the being itself. There were things all around him, but he simply couldn't process any of it in a comprehensive way. Colors didn't appear in their customary way, as light seemed to be a physical aspect of this separate universe; all particle and no wave. Light came from everything. It had shape and shone in different shades of brightness with no logical pattern. He saw the cache, a massive structure of metal and glass teeming with gateways to other galaxies, and the Helios and the Harvester resting near the edge of one of the wormholes. Nolan couldn't determine if he was in space or on a surface somewhere, but he could breathe, and felt an even stronger connection to emotions coming from somewhere other than the being he was fighting. It felt as if he was amid many beings, but also linked to these beings. A sense of fear dominated this space, seemingly generated by his hostile enemy. Nolan sensed that a tremendous upheaval of the natural order of this dimension stemmed from the cache, which was something the scientists on the other side of the interdimensional bridge never took into consideration.

Whatever attempt Nolan had intended to make to contain or eliminate the fourth dimensional threat was quickly revealed as an extreme improbability, because this being wasn't just a single entity lurking about the cache. It was a legion. In a snap judgement, he decided to make his best effort to get the Helios back to the control station, and hopefully hold this endless enemy off long enough so that the others could board it and head for safety.

He made a move toward the shuttle, only to be halted by a massive attack. Nolan felt a thousand fists hammer him. He punched, grabbed, and kicked at anything and everything that seemed to be on him or near him. Surprisingly, it had an effect. He felt contact when he swung. He was able to put his hands on he-knew-not-what and throw it. The being was able to hold Nolan and hit him hard, hurting him, but he didn't feel anything like what Doctor Wu had described in his own encounter. As much of a beating as the beings could give, Nolan could take it. There was pain, but it was bearable. There were punches so hard they defied his understanding of force, but he endured them, dispatching his own in retaliation.

Regardless of his adept fighting abilities, Nolan felt he was in a fight that could rage on for eternity. He still needed to get Armstrong and Raincloud across the hyperspace bridge, and back to the team. As he started to move toward the Helios again, he carried the onslaught with him, as though he wore it like a suit. Blow after blow covered his body as though it was his own skin, and each strike stretched his insides as though they were his own bones pulling on him. He kept hitting back, pushing, biting, and throwing whatever he could get hands on.

As they fought, they moved along the edge of the cache, near the open wormholes filled with other galaxies and solar systems. Stars and planets, some possibly flourishing with life, flashed their light through the wormholes onto the battle as it raged on. While fighting, Nolan couldn't shake the feeling that his enemy was suffering, and that it was due to its world having been upended. Nolan realized that he, along with the wormhole cache, were nothing more than a disruptive occupation of someone else's home, and that this fighting was an invasion.

He stopped fighting, sensing the being's impulse that made it fight for its life. He now hoped it would empathize with him. He continued to move toward Armstrong and Raincloud in the Helios, enduring a beating along the way. When he finally reached it, he grabbed hold of the arm latched to the Harvester and broke it in half. He then lifted the Harvester up by the broken arm and swung it around over his head, building up momentum as it spun. He let go of it, and watched as it passed through the hyperspace bridge, back toward the control station in the third dimension. He then grabbed hold of the Helios and with all his power pushed it out of the fourth dimension, sending it back across the hyperspace bridge into the space near the control station where the team would be able to board it and escape. As he did so, his enemy doubled down on him with raging aggression, finally wrestling him into submission. Held by a force greater than any he'd ever known, he began to charge, preparing to teleport away from the fight. As the electricity began to form around him, the legion battling him absorbed the energy, and instantly redirected it into Nolan. The shock was powerful, amplified by his enemy before it was released back onto him. It weakened him to the point where he could no longer fight back.

The enemy then reached across the hyperspace bridge and into the third dimension. It grabbed the Helios again along with the control station and dragged them both across the hyperspace bridge into the fourth dimension. The control station began to break apart as it was pulled in. Pieces scattered as debris spread throughout both dimensions and into countless wormholes in the cache. The Helios also disappeared into a wormhole. A shockwave was released when the core hull of the control station was destroyed, which hit the cache, causing another massive explosion that flew out in all directions in both dimensions; a blue ring of cosmic energy. When the energy from the explosion cleared, everything around it was gone. The explosion, the control station, and the cache all ceased to be, erased from time and space forever. Nolan, the team, the connection to the fourth dimension, and every other troubling thing orbiting Venus disappeared without a trace.

48

Earth, like the people on it, was running on empty. Everything other than humans, and the vermin living off them in the refugee camps, had died off. Emilia Trust identified with the vermin. Eli granted her food, comfort, and the few luxuries still available on the cold, dark planet, in exchange for delivering reports to the refugee camp on his behalf.

A stream of pro-Quest soundbites and video content aired continuously in the camp to celebrate mankind's newest savior, Eli Quest. The propaganda was always prepared for her. Her daily report to the refugee camp existed solely because Eli wanted it to. QuestCorp's public relations machine crafted all the content, and every night her voice and smile went out across the screens, but there was little truth in her words. At the end of the day she was just another hack trying to score a meal, but instead of wading in the squalor of a tent city she had butler service and a room in the north wing of QuestCorp's headquarters. When she thought about it, it made her sick. More often than not, she didn't think about it.

Speaking with Eli on a video conferencing call about her latest story to report, he sent her the information with a peculiar delight that she'd never before seen. The content was complete with "actual footage." It was too much for her. She broke down into sobs, collapsing on the floor of her room. "This is impossible," she said to Eli through the video monitor. "It's outlandish and rank with falsehoods. I am not reporting this!"

Eli responded. *"Miss Trust, let me remind you of our arrangement. Report the story, or be turned out into the darkness,* beyond the refugee camp. S.W.A.R.M. will personally escort you to the edge of civilization."

The video feed went black. She sat up and adjusted herself at the desk. S.W.A.R.M. positioned a camera in front of her and switched it on.

"Good evening, I am Emilia Trust, and thank you for watching the QuestCorp Daily Report. Tonight, we revisit a story that hit like a ton of bricks last month, when Savior and a small band of rebel fighters attacked the QuestCorp facility in Western Europe, stealing one of the company's space shuttles used to transport hydrogen from storage in Moon City to its food and energy production facilities around the globe. In our footage, you can see Savior and the rebel fighters wreaking havoc on QuestCorp's Semiautomated Worker Automaton Relief Management operation, commonly referred to as S.W.A.R.M. Savior appears to be destroying the robots used primarily as a relief platform for people all over the world, handling food distribution as well as finding people lost out there in the dark. Savior can be seen literally tearing the robots to pieces while helping armed rebels hijack the shuttle and fly off into space with it.

An update to that ongoing story came from QuestCorp today. Savior and his rebel band have destroyed the ICS, or the Interstellar Control Station, which is used by the company to create and manage wormholes in space. In a statement from Eli Quest, he revealed that he was working on a solution to Earth's ongoing plight that involved the use of wormholes, but now that endeavor is put off indefinitely.

The motives for the unprompted attacks are unclear, but what is clear is that Savior, recently revealed to be an alien hiding among us by a QuestCorp investigation, and the attackers have served a significant blow to QuestCorp's worldwide humanitarian support efforts. With now only one shuttle to transport hydrogen to Earth from the Moon for the company's nonstop food production schedule, the company's food and energy programs can now only be supplied at fifty percent capacity. As a result, QuestCorp has initiated emergency protocols in an attempt to thwart a massive starvation event. On the one hand, it is working around the clock to finish its second-generation shuttles, which have been in the works for some time. On *the other hand, in an effort to prioritize the use of hydrogen to produce food while the company completes its new rockets, QuestCorp will temporarily stop producing hydrogen-fueled power. Starting immediately after this broadcast, all power systems not related to necessary QuestCorp programs or food production will be shut down, and their hydrogen fuel will be redirected for use by the company's food programs. As of this moment, Eli Quest is busy leading the emergency relief effort, and is therefore unavailable for further comment, but in his release stated that while there was no timeframe in place, he would personally see to it that the people of Earth would be saved, and that this recent attack by Savior is what he considers to be the greatest blow to humanity the world has ever seen.*

While most of us will be left in the cold and the dark wondering why Savior, someone who had been a hero and a symbol of hope for so long, would attempt to destroy QuestCorp's ability to save the people of Earth, Elijah Quest will be working endlessly to right this wrong and save mankind from the egregious acts by what has turned out to be Earth's greatest villain. Mister Quest has vowed to hunt down Savior wherever he is and bring him to justice on behalf of all mankind after the new shuttle is brought online and food and power production has resumed in full. As for this reporter's thoughts, in looking ahead to a brighter future free from the nightmare of endless night, all hope is lost. I'm Emilia Trust. Thanks for watching, and good luck to you all. Goodnight."

Ending the broadcast with her own thoughts was not part of Eli's script, but she couldn't resist the urge. She was certain there would be heavy-handed repercussions for her actions, but it was the only way she could get through her report without gagging. As soon as the cameras turned off, S.W.A.R.M. grabbed her, and took her away.

49

Eli was returning from a drone transport tour of the Moon. As he docked the vehicle, he called his assistant on the comm. "Fergus, the fix on the battery is holding. Replace the lunar rovers with the drones and inform the staff."

"*Yes, sir.*"

"I want to meet with Li Wei to discuss the timeline for his wormhole production. I'll meet him in my office. Send him now."

"*Yes, sir.*"

Eli docked and exited the drone. As he walked out of the ship bay he was grabbed by his shirt and thrown against a wall. He hit the back of his head and fell to the floor. Stunned, he couldn't gain focus or turn to see who had attacked him before he was picked up by his shirt again and thrown once more. He flew through the air, this time landing on the floor facedown. He rolled to his side, dazed, and coughed as he struggled to catch the wind that was knocked out of him. He was picked up again, this time by the back of his neck.

"Stop! Stop! Please!" He pleaded.

He was turned around and dropped into the chair of a nearby table. It knocked the wind from him again.

"Eli Quest," his attacker said.

Eli tried to focus on the man. It came slow, but Eli zeroed in on the man's face. "Who are you? What do you want?" As he spoke, a small trail of blood dripped from the corner of his mouth. The large man stood directly in front of him.

"My name is Sylas Green. I knew your father."

Eli put his hand to his face in between his eyes, taking a minute to breathe and get himself centered. "Knew?"

"Your father is dead. He died waiting for you."

Eli focused, and looked Sylas in the eyes. "He would've known better. What really happened?"

Sylas hmphed, and then smiled. "He told me you were gonna come and get us."

Eli sat, stunned.

Sylas continued. "I came up here with him one time. I remembered how we did it. It's nice up here."

Eli looked to the wall near the exit where an emergency call button was placed. Sylas saw him and looked as well. "That a panic button or something? Well, don't worry. That was for not taking care of your Dad. I'm not gonna hit you again."

"What are you going to do?"

Sylas smiled, looked down, and nodded, before looking eye to eye with Eli and smiling. "It's nicer up here than down there."

"You want to stay here."

"Yeah. I do. I have skills, Mister Quest. I can be useful."

Eli feigned interest. "Really? What kind of skills do you have?"

"The kind of skills someone who'd let their father die on a dead planet might find valuable. You're cold, Mister Quest. I'm cold too."

Eli started to laugh. It started out quiet but quickly became loud and boisterous. "What makes you think I need someone like you?" He asked through the laughter. "I have a robot legion to do my bidding, and a league of scientists that can destroy worlds. Why would I need an arrogant, overambitious thug with a 'cold' side to help me with anything?"

Sylas smiled and laughed along. "I don't really know, I guess." Then his face grew serious as he gazed out to the lunar landscape through the ship bay. "But it's nicer up here than down there. And, I'm not going back. I remember that group of fellas that got to you back on Earth. That siege of your facility at the refugee camp. I was there; not in the fight, but in the camp. I figured you'd leave after something like that. I figured you'd come back up here. I decided I would too."

"My security will discover you are here. What chance do you think you have?"

Sylas opened his jacket, revealing a crude bomb he had rigged. It had a pull-string detonator. "They might find me. They might not," he said. "They might not find either of us." He opened the other side of his jacket and pulled a handgun from it, aiming at Eli' face. "All I have to do is head over to those hydrogen tanks with you and BOOM!"

Eli's eyes widened as he listened more seriously. He looked again at the wall, to the alarm only ten feet from him. Sylas smiled again.

"Push it. Go ahead. See what happens. Your robot army is on Earth. Your scientists can't stop bullets, and I'll put a bullet in your skull long before your security gets here. So, what do you got? What's that button gonna do for you?"

"What do you want?"

Sylas picked Eli up out of his chair and pushed him to the ground. He sat down in the chair and kicked his feet up onto the table. "Well," he said. "What do you got?"